☀ **Reading Power 系列**

Intermediate

英文閱讀
High Five

附翻譯與解析

王隆興

學歷：淡江大學美國研究所碩士
　　　國立中央大學英美語文學系學士
經歷：臺北市立南港高中英文教師

三民書局

序

知識，就是希望；閱讀，就是力量。

在這個資訊爆炸的時代，應該如何選擇真正有用的資訊來吸收？
在考場如戰場的競爭壓力之下，應該如何儲備實力，漂亮地面對挑戰？
身為地球村的一分子，應該如何增進英語實力，與世界接軌？

學習英文的目的，就是要讓自己在這個資訊爆炸的時代之中，突破語言的藩籬，站在吸收新知的制高點之上，以閱讀獲得力量，以知識創造希望！

針對在英文閱讀中可能面對的挑戰，我們費心規劃 Reading Power 系列叢書，希望在學習英語的路上助你一臂之力，讓你輕鬆閱讀、快樂學習。

誠摯希望在學習英語的路上，這套 Reading Power 系列叢書將伴隨你找到閱讀的力量，發揮知識的光芒！

給讀者的話

在學科能力測驗中閱讀測驗與混合題型，兩者約佔整分試卷分數三分之一，比例不可謂不重。讀者如能掌握閱讀測驗與混合題型分數，就能掌握先機，成功一大半。

理論上，如果通篇閱讀測驗都能理解，答題就易如反掌，分數就能手到擒來，但實際上大多數讀者都力有未逮。故必須經由考前一次次的反覆練習來提昇閱讀能力，進而能在考場上「克敵制勝」。本書之誕生即是要幫助讀者達成此一目的。

進行閱測作答時建議參考以下三項原則：

1. 注意文章第一段。第一段通常會陳述本文的主旨，瞭解第一段大意幾乎能掌握全文所要傳遞的訊息。相同的道理，理解第一段的主題句（通常為第一句）也就幾乎能掌握整個段落的大意。

2. 快速瀏覽整篇文章。快速瀏覽整篇文章會對一些重要訊息有較深刻的印象。此時可就簡單題目 (local) 先作答，如遇較困難的題目 (global)，再做詳細閱讀。

3. 如遇艱澀難懂的字句千萬別緊張。緊張只是自亂陣腳，有時這些字句並不會影響你對通篇文章的理解。最好由上下文來猜猜看語意 (word attack)，也可先瀏覽一下題目，再回過頭來找答案，通常會有出人意表的效果。

本書題材包羅萬象，舉凡生態物種、人文歷史、科學科技、環境保育、醫學保健等題材均羅列其中。希望藉由各種不同題材文章的呈現，幫助拓展讀者的知識領域，進而在考場上，對於各類型及題材的文章均能駕輕就熟，輕鬆獲得高分。書末並附詳細的翻譯與解析本，既可作為課堂教材，也極適合個人的自修精進。

欣見本書順利付梓，但實非筆者一人之力所能為，十分感謝三民書局編輯部同仁傾力協助。另，筆者才疏學淺，疏漏之處在所難免，望先進不吝指正。

王隆興

於臺北市立南港高級中學

Acknowledgments

The articles in this book are written by the following authors. The author of the book and publisher are grateful to them for their kind effort and help. All rights are reserved by San Min Book Co., Ltd.

Jamie Blackler	"The Life and Death of Stars," and "A Supermoon in the Sky"
Junita Bognanni	"The Crisis of European Refugees," and "Leonardo da Vinci—the Renaissance Man"
Jason Crockett	"Rise of the Thinking Machines"
Tracy Dery	"Fighting Fatigue"
Editage	"Man-Eating Myths"
Ian Fletcher	"The Rise of the Superweeds"
Paul Go	"Google—the Best Search Engine in the World" adapted from "Housekeeping," "Fever Helps Us Fight Diseases" adapted from "Fighting with Fever," and "Ads Add Pounds"
Jason Grenier	"Blowing Hot Air—Origins of the Filibuster," "What Happens when We Become Angry?," "Self-Driving Cars of the Future," "The Pet Rock Craze" adapted from "The Pet Rock Craze—One Genius or One Million Fools?," and "Preserving Natural Areas"
Guy Herring	"How Man's Fiercest Rival Became Man's Best Friend," "Wings—when Birds Can Only Flap, Not Fly," and "Are Animals Able to Trick Each Other? "
Helen Johnson	"The Camel Library," "How Animals Communicate," and "Should You Be Afraid of Your Food?"
Ted Pigott	"Too Much Complaining Can Do You Harm," and "Noise Pollution No More!"
Sean Sebastian	"Salmon Jump and Bears Lunch" adapted from "Salmon Stunts and Bear Brunch," "Too Busy to Be Healthy," "The Kitchens of Tomorrow," and "From Chaturanga to Chess" adapted from "Chess: from Chaturanga to Checkmate"
Sharon Shreet	"Honoring Mothers," "No More Inky Mess," "Pet Vacations," "Globesity," "Don't Toss That Phone!," "Housebreaking a Puppy" adapted from "Housetraining a New Puppy," "Keeping Our Blood Supplies Safe," and "The Cause of Floods and Droughts"
Irene Sun	"Will Digital Currencies Take Over the World?," "Climate Change and Our Mental Health," "Fighting Food Waste," and "You Can Lead a Zero Waste Lifestyle, Too"
Vanessa York	"The History of Coffee"
Maria Zinovieva	"Small Puff, Big Problem" adapted from "Small Puff—Big Problem," "The Magical Amazon River" adapted from "The Magical Amazonia?," "Tea Culture," "Pain in the Back," "The Colonial Houses," "Gopher Tortoises," "Sugar or Not?," "Living in Harmony with Your Environment," and "Another Remedy to World Hunger?"

Photo credit: Shutterstock

混合題型相關介紹

何謂混合題型？

　　為呼應新課綱強調素養、重視與生活情境結合，因而設計混合題型。旨在評量學生的閱讀能力，同一篇選文中以不只一種作答方式進行測驗（如以選擇題、填充、簡答或表格填寫），以更深入、更生活化地評量學生英文閱讀理解能力，命題上也將更有彈性。基本上，混合題型仍以評量閱讀能力為主，故評分將以答案的正確性為重，對拼字部分給予較大的空間，扣分原則不同於非選擇題的「中譯英」。學生作答應按作答說明及提示，完整而正確地回答，評閱原則交由當次考試閱卷評分標準訂定會議擬定。

（以上文字內容擷取自大考中心公布之考試說明）

以下為大考中心公布之評分原則：

給分^{備註}	評分原則說明
2 分	答案正確，語意完整。
1 分	答案不完整或不完全正確，或因拼字造成語意不清者。
0 分	空白、答案錯誤，或與答案無關之文字。
備註：以 2 分作為給分事例，實際配分及評分級距，將視正式試卷全卷狀況調整，並依當次考試評分標準訂定會議所擬定之評分原則作為評閱標準。	

資料來源：大考中心公布之「111 學年度起適用之學科
能力測驗各考科參考試卷公告（109 年 4 月
6 日更新）」（掃描下方 QR code 前往）

STEP 1 閱讀左頁文章內容，根據左頁文章內容回答右頁相關問題。

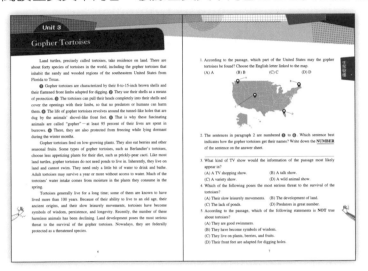

以下為書中題目類型：

1. 選擇題：根據題目說明選出正確之選項。
2. 圖片選擇題：根據題目中的圖片，選擇出正確之選項。
3. 標號題（❶、❷、❸…）：根據題目說明填入適當回答的句子號碼。
4. 勾選題：根據題目說明勾選出正確解答。
5. 表格填充題：根據題目說明於表格內填入正確解答（字詞或句型）。

STEP 2 解析夾冊內容包含：每回附文章中譯、解析及 15 個文章相關的單字補充。解析的部分採逐題說明，可於作答後進行對答。

CONTENTS

生態
物種

Unit 1	Pet Vacations	8
Unit 2	Salmon Jump and Bears Lunch	10
Unit 3	Gopher Tortoises	12
Unit 4	How Animals Communicate	14
Unit 5	Another Remedy to World Hunger?	16
Unit 6	Man-Eating Myths	18
Unit 7	Housebreaking a Puppy	20
Unit 8	How Man's Fiercest Rival Became Man's Best Friend	22
Unit 9	Wings—when Birds Can Only Flap, Not Fly	24
Unit 10	Are Animals Able to Trick Each Other?	26

人文
歷史

Unit 11	Honoring Mothers	28
Unit 12	The Camel Library	30
Unit 13	From Chaturanga to Chess	32
Unit 14	Tea Culture	34
Unit 15	Living in Harmony with Your Environment	36
Unit 16	Blowing Hot Air—Origins of the Filibuster	38
Unit 17	The Pet Rock Craze	40
Unit 18	The Crisis of European Refugees	42
Unit 19	Leonardo da Vinci—the Renaissance Man	44
Unit 20	The History of Coffee	46

科學
科技

Unit 21	No More Inky Mess	48
Unit 22	The Kitchens of Tomorrow	50
Unit 23	The Colonial Houses	52
Unit 24	Google—the Best Search Engine in the World	54
Unit 25	Ads Add Pounds	56

Unit 26	Self-Driving Cars of the Future	58
Unit 27	Will Digital Currencies Take Over the World?	60
Unit 28	Too Much Complaining Can Do You Harm	62
Unit 29	The Life and Death of Stars	64
Unit 30	Rise of the Thinking Machines	66

環境
保育

Unit 31	Don't Toss That Phone!	68
Unit 32	The Magical Amazon River	70
Unit 33	The Cause of Floods and Droughts	72
Unit 34	A Supermoon in the Sky	74
Unit 35	Noise Pollution No More!	76
Unit 36	You Can Lead a Zero Waste Lifestyle, Too	78
Unit 37	Preserving Natural Areas	80
Unit 38	Thc Risc of the Superweeds	82
Unit 39	Climate Change and Our Mental Health	84
Unit 40	Fighting Food Waste	86

醫學
保健

Unit 41	Globesity	88
Unit 42	Small Puff, Big Problem	90
Unit 43	Pain in the Back	92
Unit 44	Sugar or Not?	94
Unit 45	Fighting Fatigue	96
Unit 46	Fever Helps Us Fight Diseases	98
Unit 47	What Happens when We Become Angry?	100
Unit 48	Keeping Our Blood Supplies Safe	102
Unit 49	Should You Be Afraid of Your Food?	104
Unit 50	Too Busy to Be Healthy	106

Unit 1

Pet Vacations

Pet owners often face tough choices when vacation time rolls around. Their **furry friends** probably can't come along to the beach or the nature preserves — dogs and cats may spread diseases to wildlife, and often they don't enjoy long car rides.

❶ The German Animal Protection League has come up with an alternative. ❷ Using the slogan "You take my pet, I'll take yours," it offers a service to help pet owners take a carefree vacation. ❸ The service matches pet owners who are planning to take a trip with others who would be happy to take the travelers' pets into their homes. ❹ The owners and "pet sitters" meet to discuss the animals' needs, and the owners pay a fee to the sitters for their pets' food and care. ❺ The fee, which is set by the sitters, is usually low. ❻ Most of the pets enjoy the companionship of another family while their owners are away. ❼ When the sitters want to take a vacation, they can also use this service to find someone to care for their pets.

Pet sitting is becoming more and more popular. Many pet owners often form informal networks to care for each other's pets. One community in the United States uses social media to let residents know who is available for pet sitting. In many other communities, the messages spread by word of mouth. Krista Stephens, the owner of two dogs, hires pet sitters whenever she travels. "The boys," as she calls her dogs, "seem to enjoy the experience, and I can relax, knowing they are in good hands," she says.

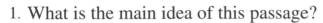

生態物種

1. What is the main idea of this passage?

(A) To give an example of how pet owners can plan a good vacation for their pets.

(B) To explain why pet trading becomes popular on the Internet in Germany.

(C) To show how travelers use newsletters to find their accommodation in the U.S.

(D) To introduce who can help take care of pets when their owners are away on vacation.

2. What does "**furry friends**" mean in the first paragraph?

(A) Pet owners.   (B) Dogs and cats.

(C) Animal lovers.   (D) Pet sitters.

3. The sentences in paragraph 2 are numbered ❶ to ❼. Which sentence best indicates what kind of service the German Animal Protection League provides? Write down the **NUMBER** of the sentence on the answer sheet.

4. According to the passage, which of the following signs may be seen at the entrance of a nature preserve?

(A)    (B)

Staff Only

(C)    (D)

5. Which of the following can be inferred from the passage?

(A) Ms. Stephens had unpleasant experiences of pet sitting.

(B) The fee which pet owners pay for pet sitting is determined by the league.

(C) Pet sitters may have their pets looked after when they travel.

(D) The matching service costs a lot and it is not a popular business.

Salmon Jump and Bears Lunch

❶ The life cycle of the sockeye salmon goes full circle and brings them into an amazing encounter with fishing bears. ❷ Born in Alaska, the two-year-old sockeye travel for a couple more years throughout the Pacific Ocean, until their instinct brings them back. ❸ In the early summer, millions of the adult salmon gather together and squeeze into the fresh water of the Naknek River, then spread out again in the huge Naknek Lake. ❹ After crossing the lake, the sockeye are nearly back to where they were born—Brooks Lake. ❺ To get there, however, it requires an enormous act of energy and bravery. ❻ They must swim through the Brooks River and throw themselves up a six-foot waterfall while avoiding the massive brown bears that come here to feed on these delicious fish.

There is a viewing platform at Brooks Falls for tourists to see the spectacle of bears waiting to feed on fish. On a visit, a tourist may see as many as 15 bears settle there and patiently await a salmon to throw itself up the falls and into their mouths. Often a salmon can't get the angle right—instead of jumping over the falls, it dives right into the falling water, and has to start over. If one leaps close enough to a bear, the bear will grab it in mid-air and swallow it, storing up fat for the long Alaskan winter. If the bear spots a sockeye in the water, it will jump headfirst into the river, holding the fish to the rocks with its giant paws, and then returning to land satisfied, with a bit of sashimi for lunch.

All of this danger in the midst of the journey doesn't stop the salmon from attempting the great leap to the calm waters of their birthplace so that they may give birth, continuing the cycle of life.

1. Which of the following posts the biggest threat to the sockeye salmon's journey back to its birthplace?

    (A) The freezing weather in Alaska.

    (B) The visitors on the viewing platform.

    (C) The massive brown bears.

    (D) The Pacific Ocean.

2. According to the passage, why do the brown bear eat the salmon?

    (A) It cannot snatch the salmon in mid-air.

    (B) It needs enough fat for the cold long winter.

    (C) It dives right into the falling water.

    (D) It throws itself up a six-foot waterfall.

3. Which of the following is **NOT** supported by the passage?

    (A) To swim back to their birthplace, the salmon need energy and bravery.

    (B) Many bears feed on salmon at Brooks Falls.

    (C) It is a tourist spectacle to see the brown bears waiting to eat the salmon.

    (D) If the bear sees a salmon in the water, it will let go of it.

4. The sentences in paragraph 1 are numbered ❶ to ❻. Which sentence best indicates what drives the salmon to return to their birthplace? Write down the **NUMBER** of the sentence on the answer sheet.

_____

5. Which of the following describes the journey that the salmon takes in its life?

    (A) Naknek Lake → Pacific Ocean → Naknek River → Brooks Falls → Naknek Lake.

    (B) Brooks Lake → Pacific Ocean → Naknek River → Naknek Lake → Brooks Lake.

    (C) Pacific Ocean → Brooks Falls → Brooks Lake → Naknek River → Naknek Lake.

    (D) Naknek Lake → Naknek River → Pacific Ocean → Brooks Falls → Brooks Lake.

Gopher Tortoises

Land turtles, precisely called tortoises, take residence on land. There are about forty species of tortoises in the world, including the gopher tortoises that inhabit the sandy and wooded regions of the southeastern United States from Florida to Texas.

❶ Gopher tortoises are characterized by their 8-to-15-inch brown shells and their flattened front limbs adapted for digging. ❷ They use their shells as a means of protection. ❸ The tortoises can pull their heads completely into their shells and cover the openings with their limbs so that no predators or humans can harm them. ❹ The life of gopher tortoises revolves around the tunnel-like holes that are dug by the animals' shovel-like front feet. ❺ That is why these fascinating animals are called "gopher" — at least 95 percent of their lives are spent in burrows. ❻ There, they are also protected from freezing while lying dormant during the winter months.

Gopher tortoises feed on low-growing plants. They also eat berries and other seasonal fruit. Some types of gopher tortoises, such as Berlandier's tortoises, choose less appetizing plants for their diet, such as prickly-pear cacti. Like most land turtles, gopher tortoises do not need ponds to live in. Inherently, they live on land and cannot swim. They need only a little bit of water to drink and bathe. Adult tortoises may survive a year or more without access to water. Much of the tortoises' water intake comes from moisture in the plants they consume in the spring.

Tortoises generally live for a long time; some of them are known to have lived more than 100 years. Because of their ability to live to an old age, their ancient origins, and their slow leisurely movements, tortoises have become symbols of wisdom, persistence, and longevity. Recently, the number of these harmless animals has been declining. Land development poses the most serious threat to the survival of the gopher tortoises. Nowadays, they are federally protected as a threatened species.

1. According to the passage, which part of the United States may the gopher tortoises be found? Choose the English letter linked to the map.

   (A) A   (B) B   (C) C   (D) D

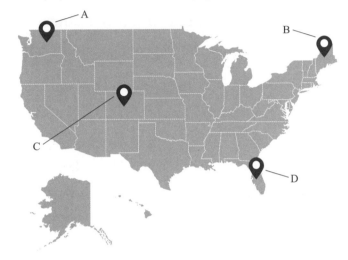

2. The sentences in paragraph 2 are numbered ❶ to ❻. Which sentence best indicates how the gopher tortoises get their names? Write down the **NUMBER** of the sentence on the answer sheet.

   _____

3. What kind of TV show would the information of the passage most likely appear in?

   (A) A TV shopping show.   (B) A talk show.

   (C) A variety show.   (D) A wild animal show.

4. Which of the following poses the most serious threat to the survival of the tortoises?

   (A) Their slow leisurely movements.   (B) The development of land.

   (C) The lack of ponds.   (D) Predators in great number.

5. According to the passage, which of the following statements is **NOT** true about tortoises?

   (A) They are good swimmers.

   (B) They have become symbols of wisdom.

   (C) They live on plants, berries, and fruit.

   (D) Their front feet are adapted for digging holes.

13

Unit 4

How Animals Communicate

❶ Animals have their inborn and unique ways to communicate. ❷ These ways may be strange and unfamiliar to us, but they are efficient and effective. ❸ For example, bees dance to communicate. ❹ After returning from a search, a scout bee will dance in a figure-8 pattern to tell the others where the latest food source is, how to get there, how long the trip will take, and the type and quality of the food.

The wildebeest also dances to communicate, but its dance means that it prefers not to be eaten this day. When pursued by a predator, the wildebeest will run fast for a short distance and then turn and face its enemy. It tosses its head from side to side and keeps on moving its legs. The predator finds itself both captivated and confused by this odd dance. It's not long before **it** abandons the prey. After all, who wants to eat a crazy wildebeest?

Yawning is also a method of communication among animals, but it doesn't mean "I'm tired." For instance, monkeys yawn to threaten their enemies. They will open their mouths wide to display their teeth to a predator or a rival monkey. For a monkey, a yawn can mean, "I bite!" Hippos also yawn, but this is to remind others just who is in charge. A hippo can open its huge toothy mouth to 150 degrees!

Animals have many other effective means of communicating, including gestures, sounds, bright colors, flashing lights, and complex scents. If you take some time to study animal communication, you will no doubt be amazed at the complexity of the world around us.

1. Which of the following is **NOT** a way of communication mentioned in the passage?
   (A) Dancing.   (B) Yawning.
   (C) Showing bright colors.   (D) Eating.

2. What does the word "**it**" in the second paragraph most likely refer to?
   (A) Wildebeest.   (B) Wildebeest's predator.
   (C) Bee.   (D) Monkey.

3. The sentences in paragraph 1 are numbered ❶ to ❹. Which sentence best indicates what kinds of information a scout bee gives in its dance? Write down the **NUMBER** of the sentence on the answer sheet.

   _____

4. What does the author use to support the idea that animals have their unique but effective ways of communication?
   (A) By giving examples found in insects and animals.
   (B) By quoting scientific reports.
   (C) By telling stories.
   (D) By comparing animals' ways of communication with humans'.

5. According to the passage, which of the following statements is true?
   (A) Hippos yawn to threaten the enemies.
   (B) Bees dance to ask their partners to return home.
   (C) Monkeys yawn to show that they will bite.
   (D) Bees dance eight times after they have found a food source.

Unit 5

Another Remedy to World Hunger?

❶ Based on a United Nation's report, genetically modified (GM) crops can become part of the solution to world hunger. ❷ However, at the moment, there is a lot of debate about whether GM crops are good or bad. ❸ Supporters of genetic engineering are saying that GM crops are easier to grow, and more nutritious, tasty and long-lasting. ❹ Vitamin and protein-enriched vegetables could improve nutrition levels. ❺ What's more, drought and insect-resistant crops might help to feed the growing world population and boost incomes of Third World countries, according to the United Nations' Food and Agriculture Organization. ❻ Countries like India, the Philippines, China, Thailand, and many more are already planting millions of acres of genetically modified crops.

On the other hand, opponents of GM foods argue that even though the cultivation of such crops can help fight world hunger, it does not really provide a comprehensive answer to this global problem. Instead, GM foods might bring more problems to Third World nations. Not only can **they** be harmful to human body in the long run, but they could also change the traditional varieties of plants through pollen exchange. They might harm the environment in a way that we fail to predict now, as the impact of GM crops has not been fully studied so far.

In Europe, consumers' opposition to GM foods on the table has been so strong that some companies had to stop the marketing of GM crops. However, many developing countries still believe in the magic of biotechnology, even though they might not have appropriate policies on controlling GM crops. World starvation has more to do with wealth distribution, rather than the inadequate production of food. In other words, what poor people really need is better access to land, markets, education, and credit systems, rather than biotechnology, which has not yet been proved good or bad for our environment.

1. Which of the following best describes the author's attitude toward GM foods?

   (A) Hopeful.   (B) Pessimistic.

   (C) Angry.   (D) Doubtful.

2. How is this passage organized?

   (A) By cause and effect.   (B) In the order of importance.

   (C) In the sequence of time.   (D) By compare and contrast.

3. What does the word "**they**" in the second paragraph refer to?

   (A) Supporters of genetic engineering. (B) European countries.

   (C) GM foods.   (D) Critics of GM crops.

4. The sentences in paragraph 1 are numbered ❶ to ❻. Which sentence best indicates the advantages of vitamin and protein-enriched vegetables? Write down the **NUMBER** of the sentence on the answer sheet.

   _____

5. According to the passage, which of the following statements is **NOT** true?

   (A) GM plants can never change the original varieties of non-GM plants.

   (B) Unequal distribution of wealth is the major cause for world starvation.

   (C) The impact of GM crops cannot be predicted now.

   (D) GM foods might do harm to human body.

17

Unit 6

Man-Eating Myths

Most people think sharks are dangerous creatures waiting to eat lone swimmers. Actually, 75 percent of all shark bites do not lead to the victim's death, and only 32 of the 350 recognized shark species have been known to attack humans! Studies conducted worldwide have led to more such discoveries.

Scientists at facilities like the ReefQuest Centre for Shark Research, Canada, have destroyed the myth of the killer shark. They found that white sharks, one of the most dangerous species, usually spit out human beings instead of eating them. Some scientists believe this is because they do not like the taste of neoprene, the rubber used in wetsuits worn by most swimmers. Others say that sharks find human beings too bony and prefer the fatty flesh of seals and sea lions.

Most shark attacks seem to have nothing to do with sharks' taste for human flesh. Their attacks are usually **prompted** by humans' invading their territory or interrupting their mating. Also, underwater, swimmers resemble seals and sea lions, and their jewelry glinting in the sun can look like fish scales. Sharks may thus attack humans they mistake for marine mammals. Another possibility is that sharks use their mouths only to find out more about objects; they bite out of curiosity rather than a desire to kill.

❶ Even if sharks do not attack human beings for food, their attacks are extremely violent. ❷ White sharks, for instance, steal up behind swimmers, biting suddenly and forcefully to inflict serious injuries. ❸ Thus, it is safest to stay clear of places where such attacks typically take place, such as channels, the mouths of rivers, and the shallow water behind sandbars near the shore. ❹ Respecting the shark's territory and ferocious power is the best way to ensure that you leave the ocean unharmed.

1. What is the purpose of this passage?

   (A) To clarify that sharks do not enjoy eating human beings.

   (B) To introduce the 350 recognized shark species.

   (C) To explain to the readers that sharks do not attack for food.

   (D) To warn the readers that white sharks are the most dangerous species.

2. Which of the following can be done for swimmers to avoid shark attacks?

   (A) To feed sharks with fatty flesh of seals.

   (B) To swim in a large group.

   (C) To wear jewelry when swimming in the sea.

   (D) To keep away from sharks' territory.

3. According to the passage, which of the following statements is **NOT** true?

   (A) Most sharks do not bite human beings to death.

   (B) Most shark species do not attack human beings.

   (C) Most sharks bite out of a desire to kill.

   (D) Attacks take place when sharks' mating is interrupted.

4. The sentences in paragraph 4 are numbered ❶ to ❹. Which sentence best indicates the places where shark attacks usually take place? Write down the **NUMBER** of the sentence on the answer sheet.

5. What does "**prompted**" in the third paragraph refer to?

   (A) Accepted.　　(B) Denied.　　(C) Caused.　　(D) Prevented.

Housebreaking a Puppy

Cuddly and soft, with big eyes, lovely paws, and a playful nature, puppies are adorable. Everyone loves them, and every year millions of people take new puppies into their homes. If you've done it, too, you know that your "puppy love" can quickly turn into frustration when you are trying to teach your pet to evacuate in the proper area. Here are some suggestions about how to train your pet, so the two of you can remain on good terms.

First, decide on a particular outdoor place for your puppy as the toilet. It'll learn more easily if you choose an area with a distinctive surface such as grass, gravel, concrete, or sand. Then, provide constant access to that area. Either set up a small pen in the area where you can leave your pet when the weather is nice, or take it outside to the special area for 45 minutes every day, rain or shine. Praise it wildly with petting and cooing, and tell it how smart and wonderful it is whenever it excretes in the proper area.

❶ During the night or when you are not at home, confine the puppy to a small area of your home. ❷ Cover the area with papers and, if possible, something that feels like the surface of your pet's toilet area—grass clippings, gravel, or sand. ❸ When the urge comes, it'll eliminate there. ❹ Be alert and never let your pet eliminate on the floor or carpet. ❺ If it intends to do so, pick it up quickly and take it to the special paper-covered spot. ❻ With time, it'll develop the habit of only relieving itself in the right area. ❼ Remember, though, no matter how hard you try, it will take at least six months for your puppy to become reliably housebroken.

1. What is the main purpose of the passage?

   (A) To demonstrate how lovely puppies are.

   (B) To give tips on how to teach puppies to eliminate properly.

   (C) To describe how to train puppies to bring you things.

   (D) To explain how our "puppy love" can turn into frustration.

2. Which of the following words in the passage is different in meaning from the other three?

   (A) Excrete.   (B) Relieve.   (C) Coo.   (D) Evacuate.

3. The sentences in paragraph 3 are numbered ❶ to ❼. Which sentence best indicates how long it takes for a puppy to become reliably housebroken? Write down the **NUMBER** of the sentence on the answer sheet.

   _____

4. Which of the following is **NOT** a suitable area for puppies as toilet?

   (A) Front yard lawn.   (B) Sandy land.

   (C) Gravel paved roadside.   (D) Household carpet.

5. Which of the following is **NOT** true about training your pet to eliminate properly?

   (A) Taking your puppy out for no more than 30 minutes every day helps train your pet.

   (B) Unsuccessful training experience can make pet owners frustrated.

   (C) A puppy needs encouragement when it relieves itself in the right place.

   (D) Puppies need constant access to the area where owners want them to excrete.

21

Unit 8

How Man's Fiercest Rival Became Man's Best Friend

❶ In today's world, dogs play an important role in people's lives. ❷ They live side by side with humans and accompany us in all parts of our lives, including hunting, herding, transportation and simply as pets. ❸ However, dogs weren't always so close to humans. ❹ Historically, dogs came from grey wolves and they used to compete with humans for food. ❺ Wolves lived in large groups and their families were similar to humans'.

Humans were a big threat to wolves, although wolves without a pack learned that if they weren't aggressive, they could get closer to humans and eat their food. These tamer wolves lived longer and this gene was passed on. They were used by humans to find people or things and to look out for danger. Slowly, wolves began to understand human commands. The first dog appeared about 32,000 years ago. They looked like wolves but had smaller body, nose, and teeth. As humans' lives changed, dogs also adapted to new environments and new jobs. Short, stocky dogs were used to herd animals; long, thin dogs helped to chase foxes out of holes; slim dogs were used for racing and finally, muscular dogs were used as guardians.

Dogs as we know them today began to appear in Victorian England. Dogs were bred for their appearance and were divided into different breeds. Today, some of these dogs suffer from health problems, such as back problems and difficulty in breathing because of this breeding. Dogs have gone through a massive change in a short time. Just as human lives have changed, so have dogs. There has been a mutual love and respect. As a result, it is likely dogs will remain man's best friend for years to come.

1. According to the passage, write down the job that will fit different shapes of dogs.

shape	job
slim	_____
short, stocky	_____
muscular	_____
long, thin	_____

2. Which of the following best describes the relationship between humans and dogs?

(A) Competitive.　(B) Unsuccessful.　(C) Cooperative.　(D) Decisive.

3. How is the second paragraph organized?

(A) By mentioning an incident.　　(B) By cause and effect.

(C) In the order of importance.　　(D) In the sequence of time.

4. Which of the following statements about modern dogs is true?

(A) They began to appear 33,000 years ago.

(B) They adapted to different jobs given by humans.

(C) They resemble their ancestors, but with larger body and sharper teeth.

(D) They are kept mainly to look out for danger or missing things.

5. The sentences in paragraph 1 are numbered ❶ to ❺. Which sentence gives us some examples on how dogs accompany us in our daily lives? Write down the **NUMBER** of the sentence on the answer sheet.

Unit 9

Wings—when Birds Can Only Flap, Not Fly

There are over 40 kinds of flightless birds that live all over the planet, including the Australian Outback, the African Savanna, and the Antarctic shores. They range from penguins, ostriches, kiwis, and emus. Despite this, these birds have found other ways of survival, such as using sharp claws to attack competitors.

❶ Being able to fly is an advantage birds have. ❷ They are able to escape danger, hunt, and travel over long distances. ❸ However, flying also causes problems, too. ❹ For example, flying consumes a huge amount of energy. ❺ In addition, it limits the body size and weight of the bird. ❻ If a bird doesn't fly, it is able to live on food with less nourishment, such as the **Takahe** from New Zealand which eats mountain grass.

If birds are under no pressure to fly, they can stop flying in a few generations. For example, if they fly to an island with no threat on the ground, they will be likely to stop flying. Their bodies change slowly over millions of years. Their bones get bigger and thicker; their back flight muscle shrinks or even disappears. Problems happen to flightless birds when humans arrive and bring other animals with them. In New Zealand, Europeans brought stoats with them, which caused many native birds to become endangered.

Large flightless birds like emus and ostriches have been flightless for millions of years, but they have survived due to their size, weight and muscles which help them run. So, if birds can't fly, what do they do with their wings? These birds have adapted their wings for other uses. Penguins swim well with them, and kiwis shelter their eggs with them. So even though these birds can't fly, they can still succeed.

1. The sentences in paragraph 2 are numbered **❶** to **❻**. Which sentence best indicates the advantages of birds' being able to fly? Write down the **<u>NUMBER</u>** of the sentence on the answer sheet.

_____

2. Which of the following can be inferred from this passage?

   (A) Human activities pose a great threat to the population of some flightless birds.

   (B) Flying birds tend to be larger and heavier than flightless birds because the former live on more nutritious food.

   (C) Stoats were beneficial to the population growth of native New Zealand birds.

   (D) When birds stop flying, their wings will become bigger.

3. Where does this passage most likely appear?

   (A) A life style magazine.   (B) An animal documentary.

   (C) A tourist brochure.   (D) A science textbook.

4. Why is "**Takahe**" mentioned in the second paragraph?

   (A) To prove what flightless birds can do with their wings.

   (B) To show how flightless birds keep their young warm throughout a cold winter.

   (C) To describe how birds' bodies slowly change when they stop flying.

   (D) To give an example of how flightless birds need less energy than flying birds.

5. Which of the following is **NOT** mentioned as an example of flightless birds?

   (A) Penguins.   (B) Emus.   (C) Stoats.   (D) Kiwis.

Unit 10

Are Animals Able to Trick Each Other?

Animals and people are said to be similar, but just as humans can be cunning and lie to each other to get what they want, can animals do the same? Male fireflies light up to attract females; yet a female firefly of another species flashes back at the male to trick it into coming closer in order to eat it. Scientists have been studying if some animals are trying to trick others. There are three steps to make sure. First, one animal must successfully fool another. Second, the animal must gain some benefit from the action. Third, the action mustn't be an accident.

Animals use different ways to cheat each other. Some animals such as the Leaf-tailed gecko and the Octopus blend into their surroundings, so other animals can't see them. This is called camouflaging. Other animals like the Scarlet King snake have adapted over generations to have stripes like the Eastern Coral snake, which is highly poisonous. This makes other animals misunderstand that they are highly toxic and stay away from them. This is known as mimicry. Another way animals try to trick each other is to change their behavior. For example, when Chameleons know that birds are near; they change color to vanish into the background.

The Fork-tailed drongo is another animal that uses a unique way to trick others. They sound an alarm to warn other animals about approaching danger. Sometimes they raise a false alarm, and the real reason for using it is to steal food from other animals. If you watch their behavior and the result, you can quickly learn their true motivation.

1. Look at the picture on the right, how do we call such a behavior?

    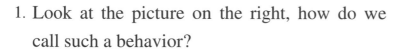

    (A) Attracting other species.

    (B) Camouflaging.

    (C) Flashing.

    (D) Sounding the alarm.

2. According to the passage, which of the following is **NOT** mentioned as a motivation for animals to trick each other?

    (A) They trick others in order to steal food.

    (B) They trick others in order to avoid predators.

    (C) They trick others in order to attract their next meals.

    (D) They trick others in order to attack their habitats.

3. Which of the following statements is true about the Scarlet King snake?

    (A) They are highly poisonous.

    (B) They change color to vanish whenever predators approach.

    (C) They have evolved to have stripes similar to a kind of poisonous snake.

    (D) The male snakes raise a false alarm to attract females.

4. How does the author conclude the first paragraph?

    (A) By giving a definition.   (B) By telling a story.

    (C) By quoting a science report.   (D) By mentioning a documentary.

5. According to the passage, write down the information we can find about Chameleons and Fork-tailed drongos.

	unique ways of tricking others	purposes
Chameleons	_____	to avoid birds
Fork-tailed drongos	raising a false alarm	_____

Unit 11

Honoring Mothers

Mothers hold a special place in the hearts of people all over the world, and many places have a special day to honor them.

1 The earliest celebrations for a mother were part of an ancient Greek festival to welcome the coming of spring and honor Rhea, the mother of the gods. **2** Later, during the 1600s, people in England developed a custom to celebrate "Mothering Sunday." **3** People were usually given the day off so that they could visit their "Mother Church," which was the main church of the area. **4** It was considered important to return to their Mother Church once a year and reunite with their own mothers and other family members. **5** Eventually, Mothering Sunday became a day for people throughout Europe and the British Isles to honor both the Church and their mothers.

In the United States, a woman named Ana Jarvis proposed that a special day be set aside to honor mothers throughout the nation. She wrote to churches and business leaders across the country to encourage them to celebrate Mother's Day in their communities. On May 10, 1908, the first Mother's Day was celebrated in her hometown of West Virginia. The holiday then became widespread, and in 1914, the second Sunday in May was named as the United States' official Mother's Day.

Mother's Day is also celebrated in many other countries, including Sweden, Mexico, Australia, Japan, China, Canada, Singapore, and so on. Young children and adults celebrate this special day with their mothers, giving them gifts of flowers and candy to thank them for their love and kindness.

1. What is the passage mainly about?

   (A) A Greek mythology about Rhea.

   (B) The perfect gifts for mothers.

   (C) The history of Mother's Day.

   (D) The countries celebrating Mother's Day.

2. Look at the calendar. Jane and Jay are planning to throw a celebration party for their mother and grandmother on the day before Mother's Day. What date will it be? Please check (✓) the appropriate box.

   ☐ May 12.

   ☐ May 13.

   ☐ May 19.

   ☐ May 20.

3. Which of the following can **NOT** be inferred about "Mothering Sunday"?

   (A) British people tend to visit the "Mother Church" on this day.

   (B) People would be granted to have the day off to be with their mothers.

   (C) The Europeans honor their mothers on this day.

   (D) It was first celebrated in the United States.

4. The sentences in paragraph 2 are numbered ❶ to ❺. Which sentence best indicates who Rhea is? Write down the **NUMBER** of the sentence on the answer sheet.

   _____

5. According to the passage, which of the following statements is **NOT** true?

   (A) The earliest celebrations for mothers were connected with the coming of spring.

   (B) Mother's Day is celebrated in many continents including Asia and Australia.

   (C) West Virginia was the first to name the second Sunday in May as Mother's Day in 1908.

   (D) Ana Jarvis encouraged business leaders to celebrate Mother's Day.

Unit 12

The Camel Library

Would you take a book from a camel? In Kenya, the national library service had organized a mobile library to reach remote villages. They used camels that can travel to where vehicles couldn't. But where did the idea of a camel library come from?

Kenya's government formed the Kenya National Library Service (knls) in 1965. Since the majority of Kenya's population lived in remote villages instead of cities, it didn't take long to see the need for a mobile library. Therefore, the organization assembled many mobile libraries with heaping boxes of books on bicycles, motorcycles, cars or trucks. The goal was to raise the country's literacy rate.

However, Kenya's North Eastern Province had never been a very safe place. Robbery along the highways was so common that motorists were advised to team up when traveling. School books were so precious that even bandits will rob elementary schools. The police have to be stationed at the entrance to each town, protecting it from being attacked by these thieves. In places like Garissa, the danger was coupled with rough terrain which even the hardiest vehicles couldn't reach.

❶ So in 1996, Wycliffe Oluoch, the Garissa librarian, organized the first camel library with three camels: one to carry a load of many books, another to carry the tent and librarian's desk, and the other camel for emergencies. ❷ Camels easily adapted to harsh weather and rugged landscapes and could walk a very long distance with little water. ❸ Each community must be qualified for a visit from the camel library: ❹ The community must be a permanent, not temporary, settlement. ❺ There must be a school with a full-time principal and teachers who would be responsible for the books. ❻ If the community lost a book, it would lose access to the library.

For many kids in Kenya, the camel library brought them the first books they have read outside the classroom. Some children enjoyed classics novels. Others liked books on science and arithmetic. The camel library had helped spread knowledge among the country step by step, giving new hope to places that were previously unreachable.

1. Which of the following statements best describes a camel library?

   (A) It is a library in which all books are about camels.

   (B) It is a library and a market where camels get together.

   (C) It is a mobile library which books are carried by camels.

   (D) People ride on camels to the library to borrow books.

2. Which of the following can be inferred from this passage?

   (A) Kenyans travel merely by camels.

   (B) The camel library is very precious to Kenyans.

   (C) Kenyans don't like to read books.

   (D) The literacy rate in Kenya is dropping rapidly.

3. According to the passage, why do the police have to be stationed at the entrance to each town?

   (A) They intend to keep the town from being robbed.

   (B) They want to stop motorists from racing on highways.

   (C) They need to prevent children from robbing books.

   (D) They advise camel riders not to go to cities.

4. The sentences in paragraph 4 are numbered ❶ to ❻. Which sentence best indicates the person behind the creation of the camel library? Write down the **NUMBER** of the sentence.

   _____

5. Which of the following statements is **NOT** supported by the passage?

   (A) Most Kenyans do not live in cities.

   (B) The northeast of Kenya has been considered not safe.

   (C) Each of the three library camels carries lots of books.

   (D) Kenyans set up camel libraries because there are places in the country that vehicles cannot reach.

Unit 13

From Chaturanga to Chess

❶ Chess has been played all over the world for centuries, but its origins are obscured by the weight of history. ❷ It is known that Indians played a similar game called "chaturanga" in the sixth century, and this is the likely ancestor of the modern game of chess. ❸ It may have spread to Europe and the rest of the world through the cultural interchanges between India and Persia or due to the Arab invasion of Persia and part of Mediterranean Europe. ❹ Over the next millennium, the game kept evolving but retained its overall characters that we know today.

King, queen, bishop, knight and pawn are chess pieces that represent the social ranks in the medieval European society. The chessboard can be used as a metaphor representing the European society in the Middle Ages. Each kind of chess pieces has its own way of moving and few exceptions are allowed.

It was played mostly by noblemen back then; they were given training in their military skills and attack strategy by performing the mathematical analysis needed to win the game. Nowadays, chess is **not a noble game anymore**. It has become a widely popular pastime and a serious competition among average people. While many of the historical references might be lost in today's chess players, the same strategies used by medieval aristocrats are still practiced by the twenty-first century players. The objective of every player is the same: checkmate, which is the winning situation when an opponent's king is under threat of capture and has nowhere to escape. In real life, this would be the end of an empire. In the game, the losing player may resign, saving the king from the humiliation of defeat. This might be the most different part between the game and the real life.

1. The sentences in paragraph 1 are numbered ❶ to ❹. Which sentence best indicates the ancestor of the modern game of chess? Write down the **NUMBER** of the sentence.

---

2. When the winning situation "checkmate" happens, which of the following chess pieces will have nowhere to go based on the passage?

(A) The king.   (B) The knight.   (C) The bishop.   (D) The pawn.

3. What does the author mean by "**not a noble game anymore**" in the third paragraph?

(A) Playing chess is despised by the royal family and the upper class.

(B) Chess games are not recognized as international events.

(C) Chess is widely played among the general public.

(D) The modern game of chess is very different from it used to be in the Middle Ages.

4. According to the passage, which of the following is the least likely reason that chess spread worldwide?

(A) The Indians conquered the Arabs.

(B) The Arabs took over Mediterranean Europe.

(C) The Arab invasion of Persia.

(D) The cultural interchanges between India and Persia.

5. Which of the following is **NOT** true?

(A) Chess is a millennium-old game.

(B) The chessboard represents medieval European society.

(C) The noblemen played chess to train their military skills.

(D) The historical references of chess are widely known by modern chess players.

33

Unit 14

Tea Culture

Tea has always played an important role in Chinese life. People's passion for it has inspired many prominent works of art. Legendary poets, such as Li Bai, Du Fu, and Bai Juyi, created quite a few poems about tea. Famous painters Tang Bohu and Wen Zhengming even drew pictures dedicated to this beverage.

❶ Before the eighth century A.D., Chinese tea was primarily used as a medicine. ❷ The tea leaf contains a number of chemicals that are known as powerful cures for inflammation and soreness. ❸ It also contains stimulants to digestion and the nervous system. ❹ Tea gradually evolved into a common beverage during the Wei, Jin, and Southern and Northern Dynasties. ❺ Later, during the Tang Dynasty, tea became an inherent feature of the society. ❻ Specialized tea tools were used and books about teas were published, including the most famous *The Classic of Tea* by Lu Yu. ❼ Tea planting and processing techniques advanced quickly. ❽ Many famous teas were, therefore, developed. ❾ There are dozens of tea types nowadays, such as Oolong, Pu-erh, Longjing, and many others. ❿ Through trading, Chinese tea spread all over the world.

Today, Chinese tea is not only a beverage, but also an important part of Chinese culture. People pay great attention to their tea and the way they drink it. They have strict requirements for the quality of the prepared tea leaves, the water they use to brew the tea, and the ware they use to serve it. A cup of tea is an essential element during a friendly talk, a family gathering, or an important business meeting. In short, tea has been a widely-beloved treasure for centuries.

1. The sentences in paragraph 2 are numbered ❶ to ❿. Which sentence best indicates as what tea was primarily used in the very beginning? Write down the **NUMBER** of the sentence.

_____

2. According to the passage, which of the following Chinese artists is **NOT** mentioned to write poems about tea?

   (A) Tang Bohu.   (B) Du Fu.   (C) Li Bai.   (D) Bai Juyi.

3. According to the passage, when was *The Classic of Tea* published?

   (A) In the Jin Dynasty.

   (B) In the Tang Dynasty.

   (C) In the Southern and Northern Dynasties.

   (D) In the Han Dynasty.

4. Which of the following statements is **NOT** supported by the passage?

   (A) The tea leaf has elements helpful for digestion.

   (B) Lu Yu wrote a book about teas called *The Classic of Tea*.

   (C) The tea leaf contains a powerful cure for inflammation.

   (D) Water plays a minor role in the making of high-quality tea.

5. Which of the following can be inferred from this passage?

   (A) The Chinese pay little attention to the tools they use to make tea.

   (B) Tea becomes a part of daily life in Chinese society.

   (C) In China, tea is served only in business meetings.

   (D) Chinese tea became a common beverage before the eighth century A.D.

Unit 15
Living in Harmony with Your Environment

❶ "Having problems with your career or troubles in your love life? ❷ The root of your problems may be in the design of your home," say the followers of the ancient Chinese philosophy—Feng Shui. ❸ Feng Shui specialists believe that everything has "Qi," energy that affects the environment and humanity. ❹ According to the philosophy, there are five kinds of Qi: metal, wood, water, fire, and earth. ❺ Different combinations of these elements will have a crucial effect upon our relations with the environment. ❻ The ultimate goal of the Feng Shui philosophy is to achieve harmony between human beings and their environment.

A major practice of Feng Shui is arranging things surrounding us so that "Qi" can be most desirable. It deals with not only the planning of cities, villages, and buildings but also the interior design. The philosophy recommends, for example, having green plants and beautiful decorations to make your environment pleasant, or keeping your house and workplace clean and clutter-free. Dust and dirt can harm your health and reduce your working ability. Another piece of advice is having the right furniture arrangement. For instance, don't sleep or sit with your back to the door. It originates from those times when people lived in fear of a wild animal or an enemy coming through the door. We still have that instinct of being uncomfortable when we can't observe the entrance while we're resting.

Today, Feng Shui is widely practiced not only by Chinese, but also by Westerners across the globe. Many celebrities, like Bill Gates and Madonna, have become fans of Feng Shui. Banks and office buildings, such as the famous Trump Tower, are built and decorated according to the principles of this ancient Chinese philosophy. Books on Feng Shui are sold worldwide, and Feng Shui consultants have their offices in many western cities. People all over the world turn to Feng Shui to make the best use of Qi, and bring peace and harmony to their mind and surroundings.

1. What is the main idea of this passage?

    (A) Westerners have become aware of the Chinese philosophy.

    (B) The philosophy of Feng Shui is to live harmoniously with one's environment.

    (C) Feng Shui is only practiced by the Chinese.

    (D) "Qi" helps defeat wild animals or enemies.

2. Which of the following statements is **NOT** true about Feng Shui?

    (A) It's about our relations with the environment.

    (B) It's an ancient Chinese philosophy.

    (C) It's only practiced by celebrities.

    (D) It helps us achieve harmony with our environment.

3. The sentences in paragraph 1 are numbered ❶ to ❻. Which sentence best indicates the elements of "Qi" ? Write down the **NUMBER** of the sentence.

_____

4. According to paragraph 2, which of the following is **NOT** having the right furniture arrangement?

    (A) A   (B) B   (C) C   (D) D

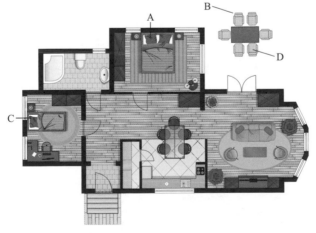

5. How is the information about Feng Shui organized in paragraph 2?

    (A) By explaining the relationship between Qi and the working environment.

    (B) By giving examples of how Feng Shui is practiced in people's daily lives.

    (C) By telling the author's personal experience of practicing Feng Shui.

    (D) By comparing the responses from Chinese people and Westerners to this ancient Chinese philosophy.

Unit 16

Blowing Hot Air — Origins of the Filibuster

U.S. senators have a history of making long-winded speeches, that is to say blowing hot air, to delay or prevent their colleagues from voting on a bill. This time-wasting strategy takes advantage of the Senate rules under which "filibuster" are allowed. As long as a senator holds the floor and keeps talking, no new business can be discussed until he or she finishes. Although there are other Senate rules to avoid filibuster, senators may take their right to speak to the extreme.

The word filibuster is said to come from a Dutch word — vrijbuiter, meaning "pirates in the Caribbean" in the sixteenth century. In the nineteenth century, "filibuster" was borrowed to describe revolutionaries and guerilla fighters, and then by the 1850s, it had taken on the meaning that it has today. The current meaning of filibuster is a metaphor for politicians "hijacking" Senate debates with long speeches.

Some politicians have been known for giving long speeches, and some filibusters have become legendary both for their length and for their pointless content. In the 1930s, Huey P. Long once held the Senate floor for 15 hours by reading the U.S. Constitution along with his favorite recipes for oysters and dumplings. Long lost the floor at last when he had to excuse himself to go to the bathroom. By far, the longest Senate speech on record was given in 1957 against the Civil Rights Act by Senator Strom Thurmond. The southern senator talked for 24 hours and 18 minutes. That's **a lot of hot air**!

1. What is the modern meaning of the word "filibuster"?

   (A) It means the description of guerilla fights.

   (B) It means the recitation of the U.S. Constitution.

   (C) It means the speech senators give to stop other senators from voting on a bill.

   (D) It means the attack that pirates make on ships.

2. When did the word "filibuster" change to its meaning today based on the passage?

   (A) 1950s.   (B) 1930s.   (C) 1850s.   (D) 1957.

3. Which of the following can be inferred from the passage about American senators?

   (A) They are not allowed to vote on a bill.

   (B) They are allowed to talk as long as they like if they can hold the floor.

   (C) They like to make short speeches.

   (D) They are known for making history.

4. Fill in the blanks with the information contained in paragraph 2 about the meaning of the word "filibuster" in different times.

	the meaning
sixteenth century	_____
nineteenth century	_____
1850s	_____

5. What does "**a lot of hot air**" mean in the last paragraph?

   (A) Statements without real meanings or truths.

   (B) Talk quickly and nonstop.

   (C) Heated debate over an issue.

   (D) A popular event.

The Pet Rock Craze

In the April of 1975, Gary Dahl, an American copywriter, was talking with friends about how inconvenient it was to keep pets like dogs and cats. He joked that a stone would make the perfect pet—quiet, well-behaved, and needing no food, water, or exercise. With this simple but original idea, Dahl invented one of the strangest fads of all time—the Pet Rock, and became a millionaire overnight.

The Pet Rock was basically an average round stone which Dahl bought for just one cent each. The stone was packaged in a box designed to look like a pet carrier with a humorous instruction manual. The instruction manual was written by Dahl himself. It included information about how to train and care for a Pet Rock, "breeds" of Pet Rocks, obedience training, and teaching them to attack.

In August, Gary Dahl began selling his "**new invention**" at gift shops. The creative packaging and humorous instruction manual captured many people's attention. In October, he was selling nearly ten thousand Pet Rocks every day. By Christmas of 1975, he had sold over one million Pet Rocks for US$ 3.95 each! Not surprisingly, by the new year, most Americans had grown tired of their Pet Rocks (they were just stones, after all) and the Pet Rock fad went like the way of all fads, disappearing as quickly as it had begun.

Many people held him up as an example of a genius. Other people looked at the Pet Rock craze and shook their heads in disbelief that so many people were willing to spend their hard-earned money on an ordinary stone.

1. According to the passage, which of the following topics may **NOT** appear in Dahl's Pet Rock instruction book?

    (A) The different breeds of Pet Rocks.

    (B) How to train a Pet Rock to obey.

    (C) How to train a Pet Rock to pee in the right place.

    (D) How to teach a Pet Rock to attack.

2. What does the phrase "**new invention**" refer to in the third paragraph?

    (A) Pet Rocks.   (B) Humorous books.

    (C) Instruction manual.   (D) Pet carrier.

3. Which of the following statements is true about Gary Dahl based on the passage?

    (A) He teaches others how to train their cats and dogs.

    (B) He became a millionaire because of the Pet Rock fad.

    (C) He was willing to spend his hard-earned money.

    (D) He thought that keeping dogs and cats as pets was convenient.

4. What can we infer from the passage about the author?

    (A) The author sells stone as pets.

    (B) The author is an expert on training stone as pets.

    (C) The author invented the Pet Rock.

    (D) The author isn't surprised that the Pet Rock fad disappeared so soon.

5. Fill in the blanks with the information contained in the passage about the reason why Gary Dahl considered a stone to be a perfect pet.

the personality traits of a stone	What doesn't a stone need to survive?

Unit 18

The Crisis of European Refugees

The Syrian Civil War has caused enormous numbers of refugees to flee across the border into Europe. As the bombing and battles continue to rage on in their hometown, tens of thousands of Syrians have found that their best chance of survival is outside their own country. Unfortunately, not all of the members of the European Union (E.U.) are welcoming the refugees with open arms.

The Syrian refugee crisis shines a harsh light on the political development among the E.U. member countries. With well-functioning systems in place to find homes and jobs for the refugees, nations like Germany, Denmark, and Sweden are willing and able to welcome more than their fair share of refugees. Some members of the E.U., including Hungary, Poland and smaller countries in the Baltic region are less willing to accommodate refugees due to fewer financial resources. **They** feel they should not be expected to take in as many refugees for fear that too many immigrants will cause conflicts among citizens. Some eastern European countries simply close off their borders when the numbers of refugees grow too high, leaving them in terrible conditions with little food and water. The unfortunate result of all this political development is that thousands of Syrians are left homeless.

While the Syrian Civil War proves that some conflicts cannot be contained, people will still do anything necessary to bring their families to safety. A worldwide effort is needed so that those in need can find shelters as soon as possible. Not only will the members of the E.U. need to work together, but other countries like the United States need to step up and help out. The Syrian refugees deserve the world's compassion. The sooner international leaders can set aside their differences, the more lives will be saved.

1. According to the passage, which European countries are in favor of helping the Syrian refugees and which aren't? Please put checks (✓) to complete the following chart.

European country	supportive attitude towards the Syrian refugees	negative attitude towards the Syrian refugees
Poland		
Sweden		
Germany		
Hungary		

2. According to the passage, which of the following statements is **NOT** true about this European refugee crisis?

   (A) Not all European Union member countries hold a positive attitude toward the refugees.

   (B) Most refugees have found their new homes in eastern European countries.

   (C) The refugee crisis has caused disagreements among European Union member countries.

   (D) The European Union shouldn't deal with this issue on its own.

3. What does "**They**" in the second paragraph refer to?

   (A) Germany.   (B) The United States.

   (C) The Baltic region.   (D) Syria.

4. According to the passage, which of the following is **NOT** mentioned as a factor affecting a European Union member country's acceptance of the Syrian refugees?

   (A) Job opportunities.   (B) Citizens' objections.

   (C) Financial resources.   (D) Language barriers.

5. What does the author mean by the last two sentences of the passage?

   (A) The Syrian refugees are in urgent need of global aid.

   (B) Leaders around the world have been in agreement about the refugees' settlement.

   (C) Saving the lives of Syrian refugees requires lots of time and money.

   (D) The Syrian refugee crisis has caused conflicts between the European Union and the United States.

43

Leonardo da Vinci—the Renaissance Man

Leonardo da Vinci was born in the small city of Vinci, Italy in 1452. He was one of the recognized geniuses of the Renaissance. He worked in many areas, including painting, sculpting, mathematics, engineering, and anatomy, among other disciplines. In honor of his achievements in multiple fields, Leonardo da Vinci is often described as **the model of "Renaissance Man."**

He is best known for his works as a painter. He created the world-famous portrait, *Mona Lisa*, which hangs in the Louvre Museum in Paris. He also portrayed a famous religious scene in *The Last Supper*, the famous wall painting in Milan. Although his inventions are not as well known, they are no less groundbreaking than his artwork. He developed the concept for the helicopter during the Renaissance, even though the technology to build one was invented centuries later. He also originated the idea of the calculator, solar power and the tank.

❶ Despite Leonardo da Vinci's enormous output of creative ideas, very few of them were realized during his lifetime. ❷ Not only did he constantly redo his projects, but he also liked to perform disastrous experimentation with painting techniques. ❸ Only a very small number of his works survive. ❹ In spite of his half-finished creations, Leonardo da Vinci's works still impact a huge number of artists, engineers, and scientists for years to come.

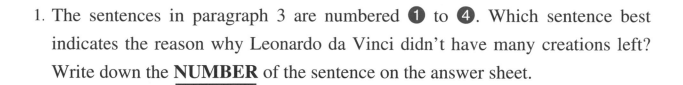

1. The sentences in paragraph 3 are numbered ❶ to ❹. Which sentence best indicates the reason why Leonardo da Vinci didn't have many creations left? Write down the **NUMBER** of the sentence on the answer sheet.

2. What does the author mean by "**the model of the Renaissance Man**" in the first paragraph?

   (A) Leonardo da Vinci was good at many things and had various interests.

   (B) Leonardo da Vinci was famous for his words of philosophy.

   (C) Leonardo da Vinci wrote many literary works in the Renaissance.

   (D) Leonardo da Vinci was an important political figure in the Renaissance.

3. What is the second paragraph mainly about?

   (A) Leonardo da Vinci and his mistresses.

   (B) The short stories about Leonardo da Vinci.

   (C) Leonardo da Vinci and his enemies.

   (D) The creations of Leonardo da Vinci.

4. Which of the following fields is **NOT** impacted by da Vinci and his works according to the article?

   (A) Aviation.　　(B) Art.　　(C) Literature.　　(D) Engineering.

5. Where does this passage most likely appear?

   (A) A fashion magazine about architecture.

   (B) A book about the renaissance geniuses.

   (C) An online article on religious education.

   (D) A brief introduction to helicopters.

Unit 20

The History of Coffee

It is believed that coffee plants originate in Ethiopia, Africa. Rumor has it that a young shepherd called Kaldi once noticed his goats eating red berries from a small, green shrub. After eating these berries, the goats danced about joyfully. Kaldi decided to try some himself. He felt energetic and clearheaded, and he danced in excitement, too. From there the effect of coffee was discovered. Coffee later spread from Africa to Arabia, where it was first roasted and made into the drink as we know it today.

❶ Coffee became an important part of Muslim culture; it was consumed to help Muslims to stay energetic and clearheaded in rituals. ❷ Wherever in the world they went, coffee went too. ❸ However, the Arab people jealously guarded the cultivation of coffee plants, and they did not allow fertile seeds to be taken out of the country. ❹ Arabia controlled the coffee industry until the 1600s. ❺ A Muslim pilgrim called Baba Budan smuggled out a few coffee seeds into India, where he started a coffee farm. ❻ Soon, coffee was being drunk in Europe, Indonesia, and the Americas as well.

Today, coffee has a special place in many cultures. People all over the world meet for coffee. Some drink it for fun while others cannot live without it. The next time you're enjoying the rich, bitter taste of a good cup of coffee, think gratefully of Kaldi and his dancing goats.

1. How does the author begin the passage?

   (A) By telling a rumor.

   (B) By giving a definition.

   (C) By asking a question.

   (D) By mentioning some scientific evidence.

2. The sentences in paragraph 2 are numbered ❶ to ❻. Which sentence best indicates which country was in control of the coffee industry before 17th century? Write down the **NUMBER** of the sentence on the answer sheet.

3. Which of the following statements about Baba Budan is **NOT** true?

   (A) He started a coffee farm in India.

   (B) He was a Muslim.

   (C) He helped spread coffee to other countries in Europe and America.

   (D) He bought coffee seeds from an Arab pilgrim.

4. According to the passage, which of the following is **NOT** mentioned as an effect caused by drinking coffee?

   (A) Being clearheaded.   (B) Talking to the gods.

   (C) Staying energetic.   (D) Experiencing excitement.

5. What is the purpose of this passage?

   (A) To introduce different coffee beans.

   (B) To show how coffee influences people's daily lives.

   (C) To explain the origins of coffee.

   (D) To teach coffee lovers how to start their own coffee farms.

人文歷史

Unit 21

No More Inky Mess

You can pay over US$ 300 for a luxury ballpoint pen or buy a dozen of them for US$ 3. You will feel great with the expensive pen in your hand. It may be decorated with silver or gold. The cheaper pens might be made of plastic and you may think that they feel light and flimsy. But when it comes to how the pens write, you'll barely notice a difference. Today's ballpoint pens, no matter how much they cost, all have a similar mechanism and can write without difficulty, but it wasn't always so.

❶ Ballpoint pens were invented in the 1930s by a Hungarian writer, László Bíró, to solve the problem of having to carry a pen and the ink separately. ❷ These first pens were filled with a tube of printer's ink and bore a tiny ball inside a cone-shaped tip. ❸ As the pen slid across the paper, the ball rotated and picked up ink from the tube, leaving it on the paper. ❹ However, the ink was pasty and thick. ❺ Writers had to press hard on the pen to get the ink to come out, or else the pen was likely to skip. ❻ If the pen was pressed too hard, its ink often came out in large amount and blotted the paper. ❼ What's worse, the pens often leaked ink, ruining the writers' clothes.

These problems were solved in 1949 when Patrick J. Frawley and Fran Seech developed a better ink and improved the pen's structure. The new ink flowed smoothly and didn't leak. In addition, it could be washed out of clothes completely. To promote his new ink, the inventor would write on retailers' shirts, offering to exchange the shirts if the ink on them wasn't removed after washing. The shirts were always able to be cleaned, so the retailers loved the ink. Within a few years, millions of these new pens were sold. To this day, we are still using ballpoint pens with the same basic ink formula.

1. What is the primary purpose of this passage?

   (A) To teach people how to tell expensive ballpoint pens from cheap ones.

   (B) To tell people about the evolution of ballpoint pens.

   (C) To let the public know how ballpoint pens are made.

   (D) To promote a newly made perfect ballpoint pen.

2. According to the passage, which of the following statements about cheap ballpoint pens is true?

   (A) They don't have a smooth flow of ink.

   (B) They skip when you write.

   (C) They would leak ink in your pockets.

   (D) They write without difficulty as the expensive ones.

3. The sentences in paragraph 2 are numbered ❶ to ❼. Which sentence best indicates the function of the tiny ball inside a ball pen? Write down the **NUMBER** of the sentence on the answer sheet.

4. Which of the following statements is **NOT** supported by this passage?

   (A) A luxury pen may be decorated with silver or gold.

   (B) In the early days, the ink inside the pen was pasty and thick.

   (C) The ink formula for ballpoint pens today is quite different from that in 1949.

   (D) Before the invention of ballpoint pens, people had to carry a pen and the ink separately.

5. Where does this passage most likely appear?

   (A) A magazine about science and life.

   (B) A study about purchasing luxuries and social status.

   (C) An advertisement about washing machine.

   (D) A history report about the invention of paper.

The Kitchens of Tomorrow

Imagine you are cooking in your kitchen, and you glance down at the counter where a digital recipe is displayed. The voice of a famous chef says, "Now add a pinch of salt and stir." You follow, and then you swipe the counter to move to the next step in the interactive cooking lesson. You then reach into the oven to take out the fish that is being cooked, but when your oven mitts contact the dish, they say, "It's not ready; just a few more minutes." This might seem like an episode in *Star Trek*, but it's actually a project at MIT's Media Lab Counter Intelligence (CI).

This small group of inventors, scientists, and researchers is focusing its intellectual energies on kitchen facilities that we use every day. Their goal is to make a smart kitchen that will help us in every way possible. For example, the refrigerator will keep track of the groceries and order automatically from the store when there is a shortage of products. A coffee cup will tell you when it's the right temperature to drink, while your knife will warn you of harmful bacteria in the food before you consume it. **These objects** work with a combination of sensors and computers to make your kitchen a more enjoyable place to work. You will be able to cook dishes you never dreamed of, and burning something in the oven would happen only in the past.

Despite the convenience they provide, these intelligent kitchen appliances might seem too costly for many people. Take the multimedia refrigerator from Korea for example. LG Electronics makes a refrigerator that allows you to watch TV or surf the Internet from a built-in monitor. The price of the multimedia refrigerator is much higher than the normal one. It's not affordable for everyone. Perhaps not too far in the future, this kitchen technology will be affordable and talking silverware and interactive video chefs will be as commonplace as blenders and microwaves.

1. What is this passage mainly about?

   (A) In the future, people can watch TV and surf the Internet in the kitchen.

   (B) An intelligent and computerized kitchen is underway.

   (C) Cooking fish in the oven is no longer a dream.

   (D) LG Electronics makes a Multi-Media Refrigerator in Korea.

2. What does "**These objects**" mean in the second paragraph?

   (A) Kitchen facilities.　　　　　　　(B) Sensors.

   (C) Computers.　　　　　　　　　　(D) Groceries.

3. Which of the following best describes the author's attitude towards the future of the intelligent kitchen appliances?

   (A) Frustrated.　　(B) Doubtful.　　(C) Amazed.　　(D) Hopeful.

4. According to the passage, write down what the following smart kitchen appliances can do.

smart kitchen appliance	usage
coffee cup	
knife	

5. Which of the following statements is **NOT** true about the smart kitchen?

   (A) Burning something in the oven might not happen.

   (B) Cooking in the kitchen will be a more wonderful experience.

   (C) Knives might not be used anymore in the kitchen.

   (D) Interactive video chefs might show you how to cook.

科學科技

The Colonial Houses

In 1750, North America was still a new world—a world dominated by the natural environment. The surroundings in which early American colonists lived were harsh, so these settlers depended on the gifts of nature and their own hard labor. Most of the settlers at that time made their living by farming. They built farmhouses in Plymouth Colony, Massachusetts, which is one of the oldest settlements founded by the colonists from England. The farmhouses there represent typical architecture of the old days.

1 Early colonial homes were made of wood because there was an abundance of trees. **2** The typical house was one and a half stories in height with a strong, wooden frame and was covered with wooden siding. **3** The furniture and kitchen tools were also made of wood. **4** The kitchen was frequently the only room with a fireplace, which provided cooking facilities and heat during the long winters, and it was the center of many home activities. **5** Colonial families were often large, so there were many activities but little privacy. **6** On one side of the ground floor was usually a hall where the family worked and ate. **7** On the other side was the room with the best furniture and the parents' bed, which was also used to entertain guests.

As time passed and populations of the colonies grew, farmhouses and their interior started to evolve into more sophisticated, less crude constructions. The style of buildings also changed, becoming more diversified as new settlers were coming from all corners of Europe. New customs and tastes in architecture were brought to the new land with them. As settlers moved west, farmhouses in every imaginable building style were constructed on the lands of the new border area. In our times, those few houses that have been preserved through the centuries remind modern Americans of the simple life of their ancestors.

1. According to the passage, where did many early colonial home activities take place?

   (A) Hall.   (B) Parlor.   (C) Kitchen.   (D) Bedroom.

2. What is the main idea of this passage?

   (A) To introduce the colonists' entertainments.

   (B) To tell us about the history of a colonial farmhouse design in America.

   (C) To predict the life of colonists in the future.

   (D) To explain the consequence of colonization.

3. The sentences in paragraph 2 are numbered ❶ to ❼. Which sentence best indicates where the room for entertaining guests will be? Write down the **NUMBER** of the sentence on the answer sheet.

---

4. According to the passage, which of the following statements is **NOT** true?

   (A) The early American settlers made their living by farming.

   (B) During the colonial period, furniture was made of wood.

   (C) The kitchen was the only room with fireplace.

   (D) Settlements were first founded in the western part of the U.S.

5. According to the passage, what may be the cause for the style of colonial houses to change dramatically?

   (A) The growing populations of farm animals.

   (B) Settlers' various backgrounds.

   (C) Industrial revolution.

   (D) Different natural surroundings.

Google—the Best Search Engine in the World

You heard a song on the street. You forgot the title of the song, but you memorized some of the lyrics. You wanted to know which song it was, but when you typed in the lyrics in the search bar of a search engine, you got one million results. You didn't know where to start. The Internet is just like a sea of information. Without a useful search engine, it is very difficult to find exactly what you want. Luckily, Google can help us open the right door—in less than 1 second.

❶ Google, a popular search engine, is the brainchild of two Stanford students, Larry Page and Sergey Brin. ❷ The success of BackRub, an earlier version of Google they invented, encouraged them to create a faster and better-organized search engine. ❸ In 1998, Page and Brin perfected the technology and started their own company. ❹ They called their new invention "Google," inspired by the mathematical term "googol," which means the figure 1 followed by a hundred zeros. ❺ The name, then, symbolizes Google's commitment to ordering the limitless facts found on the Internet.

The reason why Google is so successful is that it is completely devoted to searching. Its primary purpose is to look for things, so there are no disturbances such as ads or news on its home page. Because Google is more comprehensive and speedier than any other search engine, it provides moments of genuine surprise and satisfaction. One usually does not end up **empty-handed** when seeking an obscure essay, a long-lost childhood friend, or a unique cure for an illness on Google. The world cannot help, therefore, but keep Googling on.

1. What is the purpose of this entire passage?

   (A) To show how to use a search engine.

   (B) To present Google's inventors: Page and Brin.

   (C) To introduce the history and function of Google.

   (D) To demonstrate how Google works.

2. Which of the following statements about Google is **NOT** true?

   (A) It is a powerful search engine.

   (B) It will have ads and news on the home page.

   (C) Its earlier version was called BackRub.

   (D) It can help us find the websites we want in less than 1 second.

3. The sentences in paragraph 2 are numbered ❶ to ❺. Which sentence best indicates the origin of the name "Google"? Write down the **NUMBER** of the sentence on the answer sheet.

4. What does the author mean by "**empty-handed**" in the third paragraph?

   (A) You become lazy.

   (B) You hold nothing in hands.

   (C) You forget to bring something.

   (D) You don't receive what you expected.

5. Which of the following best describes the author's attitude towards Google's future?

   (A) Positive.　　　(B) Discontent.　　(C) Doubtful.　　　(D) Indifferent.

Unit 25

Ads Add Pounds

❶ It's only natural for children to grow bigger as they age, but now it seems they are getting bigger faster than they're growing older. ❷ The Kaiser Family Foundation (KFF), a non-profit group that monitors health issues, has found that more and more American children are overweight. ❸ Moreover, it is estimated that a majority of these overweight young people remain so when they become adults. ❹ Weight control, therefore, is a long-term problem. ❺ Typically, watching TV is blamed for childhood obesity—but the reason why watching TV makes children overweight is rather surprising.

People usually associate TV with being overweight, thinking that the more children watch TV, the more they remain inactive. Thus, they burn fewer calories and consequently gain weight. However, research suggests that childhood inactivity has little to do with being overweight. Instead, it lays the blame on TV food advertising. In recent years, food companies have focused on promoting food on kids because an average child sees more than 40,000 ads a year. It's then no wonder that children spend billions a year on food. What's more, the food commonly being sold to kids are what we call "junk food." For example chips, sodas, candies, and fast food. Companies often use popular characters to sell those fattening products: there are Spider-Man cereals and Shrek's favorite fast-food restaurant. Kids are easily influenced, and they, in turn, influence what food their parents buy.

Things can be done to stop childhood obesity: banning junk food ads, creating TV messages about nutrition, reducing the number of food ads per program, and finding outdoor activities for kids so they won't be exposed to harmful advertising all day long. "**Ads add pounds**"—maybe that's the message that should be on TV.

1. Why are Spider-Man and Shrek mentioned in the second paragraph?

   (A) To encourage children to be active like those popular characters.

   (B) To demonstrate how those popular characters give children confidence.

   (C) To give examples of how popular characters help sell those fattening products.

   (D) To tell readers how much influence movies can have on young children.

2. What can we infer from the sentence "**Ads add pounds**"?

   (A) The more ads shown on TV, the more money the companies earn.

   (B) Food ads on TV encourage children to eat more and thus get heavy.

   (C) Children are not allowed to be exposed to harmful advertising.

   (D) Ads make TV programs colorful.

3. The sentences in paragraph 1 are numbered ❶ to ❺. Which sentence best indicates what KFF is? Write down the **NUMBER** of the sentence on the answer sheet.

4. According to the passage, which of the following is the mostly to blame for childhood obesity?

   (A) Watching cartoons. (B) Childhood inactivity.

   (C) Parents and teachers. (D) TV food advertising.

5. How does the author begin the passage?

   (A) By mentioning a story.

   (B) By presenting the results of a survey.

   (C) By giving a definition.

   (D) By asking a question.

Unit 26

Self-Driving Cars of the Future

The roads can be dangerous because of speeders, drunk drivers, and drivers using cellphones while they're behind the wheel. With the number of cars increasing, traffic jams are becoming more common in big cities. One solution to all these problems may be to take the drivers out of the picture altogether and let cars do the driving themselves.

The idea of self-driving cars has been around for a long time—the question is how to overcome the technical challenges. One major problem is how to make a car "see" the road. One possible solution is to rely on a magnetic system buried in the road. Each self-driving car will have magnetic sensors installed to detect the car's position and feed that information to a control computer. Another possibility is a computer vision system, although it's easy to see how bad weather might interfere with a camera's ability to see what's ahead.

❶ Another big challenge is how to make a car "see and react" to other vehicles and objects in front of it. ❷ Two possible solutions are millimeter-wave radar and laser rangefinders. ❸ Both of these technologies are already used in the "adaptive cruise control," an active safety system that automatically adjusts the speed of the vehicle to maintain a safe distance from the vehicles ahead. ❹ Wireless communication technology might also be used to let cars continuously "talk" to one another to make sure that there is always a safe distance between vehicles.

The next big challenge is translating all this information about the road, other vehicles, and objects ahead into actual steering, speeding, and braking adjustments. In a driverless car, small and motorized controllers would have to physically replace "the driver." These motors would receive signals from the control computer and make the proper adjustments to the steering control, the throttle, and the brakes—all in the blink of an eye. In the coming days, it is possible that self-driving cars may be allowed universally, but there's still room for improvement.

1. What is the passage mainly about?

   (A) The dangers drivers might encounter when driving on the road.

   (B) Traffic jams in big cities.

   (C) The introduction to the self-driving cars.

   (D) Bad weather affecting the safety of driving.

2. The sentences in paragraph 3 are numbered ❶ to ❹. Which sentence best indicates what an adaptive cruise control is? Write down the **NUMBER** of the sentence on the answer sheet.

3. Which of the following statements is **NOT** associated with the self-driving car's ability to see?

   (A) Burying magnets in the road.

   (B) Building a computer vision system in the car.

   (C) Attaching magnetic sensors to the bottom of the car.

   (D) Installing braking adjustment devices.

4. Which of the following can be inferred from this passage?

   (A) The development of self-driving cars will fail in the end.

   (B) People can drive cars by themselves now.

   (C) Self-driving cars will appear on the road sooner or later.

   (D) The number of cars will drop gradually.

5. Which of the following statements is **NOT** supported by the passage?

   (A) Millimeter-wave radar can detect the car's position through buried magnets.

   (B) Laser rangefinders can help the car react to vehicles on the road.

   (C) Wireless communication technology can help vehicles keep a safe distance from one another.

   (D) Once the scientists conquer the technical problems, self-driving cars may become widely accepted.

Unit 27
Will Digital Currencies Take Over the World?

Humans have been using money for thousands of years, but now many people predict that the future will be cashless. They believe that bills and coins will be replaced by digital currencies, or electronic payment, such as bitcoin, Apple Pay, or PayPal. These people think that money would exist, but only in bank accounts. However, experts don't think that the future will really be a time of empty wallets and plastic cards.

First and foremost, cash is still the most reliable way to buy things. Scientists say that people value cash more than numbers in a bank account. We seem to enjoy being able to see and touch banknotes and coins. **Old habits die hard**, digital currencies still don't feel real enough to most of us. People prefer to use real money over any other alternatives.

Second, we will always need cash for emergencies. For example, in case of a power outage caused by a natural disaster, online payment won't be available; people will have to make purchases anyway. Therefore, it is close to impossible to imagine a future where we will never need cash.

Third, many people value their privacy. Cash is a legal way to make purchases without having banks tracking them. Besides, any payment in cash is completed on the spot, so buyers don't need to worry about debts or loan interest. What's more, money-saving experts also suggest that using cash helps avoid overspending because counting the bills reminds us to spend more wisely.

To conclude, paper bills and coins are here to stay. We still rely on cash more than credit cards under many circumstances.

1. What does "**Old habits die hard**" mean in the second paragraph?

   (A) People get excited when the numbers in their bank accounts increase.

   (B) People tend to keep their personal lives secret.

   (C) People like the idea of spending recklessly.

   (D) People enjoy the touch of paper bills and coins.

2. What is the purpose of this passage?

   (A) To justify the necessity of real money.

   (B) To predict the future of digital currencies.

   (C) To persuade people to use credit cards more often.

   (D) To encourage people to spend wisely.

3. Where does this passage most likely appear?

   (A) A travel brochure.   (B) An encyclopedia of science.

   (C) A financial website.   (D) A textbook of math.

4. What is the author's attitude towards the presumption that digital currencies will replace real money in the future?

   (A) Positive.   (B) Negative.   (C) Disappointed.   (D) Shocked.

5. According to the passage, what are the advantages of using real money? Please check (✓) all the appropriate boxes.

   ☐ People can buy things during a power outage.

   ☐ People can avoid overspending.

   ☐ Bank may track the records of purchases.

   ☐ People will only see the money in bank accounts.

科學科技

Too Much Complaining Can Do You Harm

❶ Have you complained about anything today? ❷ According to research, most people complain at least once a minute when they talk with other people. ❸ Why do people complain so much? ❹ Maybe it's because complaining makes them feel better. ❺ So, once people start to complain, they often begin to complain more and more. ❻ Unfortunately, other studies have shown that complaining is bad for our health.

Research has also shown that complaining can change our brains. Essentially speaking, our brains tend to work as quickly and efficiently as possible. If you do something again and again, your brain will build a strong connection with this activity. In fact, the neurons in your brain will move closer together so that you tend to do that particular activity frequently. As a result, frequent complaining actually "rewires" your brain. This means that you are likely to complain more in the future, and you may start to spend more time with other negative people. To make matters worse, researchers at Stanford University have discovered that frequent complaining can damage the brain's ability to solve problems and think intelligently. Another study has shown that frequent complaining can lead to high blood pressure and even obesity.

Fortunately, it is possible to change the habit of complaining. One way to do so is by replacing complaint with gratitude. Whenever you feel like complaining, simply think of something you are grateful for instead. Studies show that **this** can help to reduce stress and anxiety while increasing energy levels. Even though many people seem to complain every day, it is clear that cutting down on complaining can lead to several emotion and health benefits.

1. What is the purpose of the study conducted by Stanford University described in the second paragraph?

   (A) To show the connection between complaining and mental health.

   (B) To introduce several creative ways of complaining.

   (C) To encourage people to think of grateful things instead.

   (D) To prove that complaining is harmful to brain activities.

2. What does "**this**" refer to in the third paragraph?

   (A) Thinking of something we are grateful for.

   (B) Spending more time with other negative people.

   (C) Cutting down on thinking.

   (D) Solving problems and thinking intelligently.

3. The sentences in paragraph 1 are numbered ❶ to ❻. Which sentence best indicates why people complain so much? Write down the **NUMBER** of the sentence on the answer sheet.

4. Which of the following is **NOT** true about complaining?

   (A) There is a connection between frequent complaining and high blood pressure.

   (B) Frequent complaining rewires the brain to make the person complain more.

   (C) Complaining is not beneficial to increasing energy levels.

   (D) Those who complain a lot tend to feel less stressful.

5. Where does this passage most likely appear?

   (A) On a website of meditation and the spiritual world.

   (B) In a magazine on leading a healthy lifestyle.

   (C) In a study regarding social networking and personal relationships.

   (D) In a handout on safe working environment.

The Life and Death of Stars

In the universe, nothing lasts forever. Just like humans, stars have a life span of their own. Scientists believe that stars form when large clouds of gases, mainly hydrogen and helium, come together by the force of gravity. The gas then heats up and causes a chain of nuclear reactions. Usually, a star will continue to shine and give off light for millions of years. Yet eventually, the star will run out of hydrogen to use as fuel. When this happens, the star will start to expand and become a "red giant." Millions of years later, the star collapses and becomes a "white dwarf" as it is dying.

❶ Stars that are substantially larger than our sun, however, end their lives suddenly. ❷ When they run out of hydrogen, these large stars tend to blow up in a huge explosion called a supernova. ❸ A supernova can be so powerful that it shines brighter than any other star in the galaxy for a short time. ❹ After that, it rapidly fades away and a black hole is left in its place.

To this day, black holes are still one of the biggest mysteries in astronomy. Black holes pull in every stray atom and particle that is close to them. If anything enters a black hole, it can never escape. Scientists have come up with some theories about what black holes truly are. Some researchers claim that black holes are like a permanent detention hall for matter. However, other scientists believe that black holes could be the gateway to another dimension. Since gravity in the black hole is so powerful, it's believed that a person would be crushed and become flatter than his or her own shadow inside. Perhaps one day scientists will solve the riddle of black holes, but it probably won't be any time soon.

1. The sentences in paragraph 2 are numbered 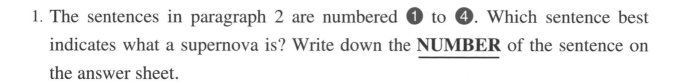 to ④. Which sentence best indicates what a supernova is? Write down the **NUMBER** of the sentence on the answer sheet.

   _____

2. According to the passage, which of the following best described the life span of a star?
   (A) Large clouds of gas → star → red giant → white dwarf.
   (B) Star → red giant → white dwarf → supernova.
   (C) Black hole → white dwarf → star → red giant.
   (D) Red giant → white dwarf → black hole → large clouds of gas.

3. What is the passage mainly about?
   (A) The life span of a galaxy.
   (B) The greatest astronomical phenomenon.
   (C) The mystery of black holes.
   (D) The birth and death of a star.

4. Which of the following statements is **NOT** true about black holes?
   (A) They come into beings after stars explode and fade away.
   (B) Anything getting into black holes can never escape from them again.
   (C) The gravity inside black holes is nearly zero.
   (D) Some people believe that black holes are the gateway leading to another dimension.

5. What is the function of hydrogen to a star?
   (A) It tells the star where to expand itself.
   (B) It serves as the fuel to a star.
   (C) It determines the size of a star.
   (D) It works as the gravity of a star.

Unit 30

Rise of the Thinking Machines

❶ In the battle of man versus machines, humans might have something to learn from their creations. ❷ An artificial intelligence (AI) computer system named Watson beat two of the best competitors ever to play *Jeopardy!*, the popular television quiz show in the United States. ❸ In a two-day tournament against Ken Jennings, who held a record for winning 74 games in a row, and Brad Rutter, who is the show's highest-earning competitor, Watson defeated its human competitors handily. ❹ The victory gave IBM, the computer's creator, a US$ 1 million prize and left humans to wonder about the meaning of Watson.

Watson is actually a collection of many IBM servers connected together to increase the system's overall capacity. This "thinking machine" uses its special software that allows it not only to understand human speech but also to precisely respond to questions in a synthesized voice. When asked a question, Watson quickly searches through its vast array of stored knowledge, such as dictionaries, literary works, and the full text of Wikipedia. It can process a million books per second and responds based on three most probable answers that it can find in the database.

During the *Jeopardy!* game, a video screen represented Watson as an avatar next to the human competitors. Unlike humans, Watson cannot leave its room at IBM and cannot work without electricity. However, the computer has an enormous advantage in the speed of pressing the button to answer questions.

Once the defeat was certain, Ken Jennings wrote a humorous message on his video screen: "I, for one, welcome our new computer overlords." However, most analysts agree that Watson's victory was good for humans. Watson's success demonstrates that AI system can be built to analyze complex problems and suggest solutions based on intricate patterns. It's a technology skill that people can use to solve challenges in various fields such as security, health care, and finance.

1. Who is Watson based on the passage?

   (A) He wins 74 games straight on a popular television quiz show.

   (B) He is an all-time money winner in the casinos of Las Vegas.

   (C) He is a senior official working for IBM.

   (D) He is an artificial intelligence computer system.

2. The sentences in paragraph 1 are numbered ❶ to ❹. Which sentence best indicates how much prize money Watson won at the quiz show? Write down the **NUMBER** of the sentence on the answer sheet.

   _____

3. What can be inferred from this passage?

   (A) Ken Jennings didn't take his defeat well.

   (B) AI system will be applied to various fields in the near future.

   (C) The *Jeopardy!* game has been removed since Watson won the victory.

   (D) Watson lives in IBM because he is bankrupt.

4. Which of the following is **NOT** true about the *Jeopardy!* game?

   (A) It is a popular television talk show broadcast in the U.S.

   (B) It offers a huge sum of prize money to its winners.

   (C) The competitors have to press the button to answer questions.

   (D) The tournament Watson played in lasted for two days.

5. Which of the following best describes the author's attitude towards the future of artificial intelligence system?

   (A) Doubtful.　　(B) Pessimistic.　　(C) Hopeful.　　(D) Conservative.

Unit 31

Don't Toss That Phone!

Your cellphone can save your life in an emergency. However, when it comes to getting a new one, your old cellphone can endanger your life and the lives of other people and animals. Millions of people discard their old cellphones every year. When cellphones are tossed into the trash, they can easily pollute the environment with poisonous materials.

Cellphones and other wireless electronic products contain dangerous chemicals such as arsenic, copper, lead, nickel, and zinc. These chemicals have been linked to cancer as well as the nervous system and reproductive disorders. If these electronic products are burned as waste, the chemicals will be released into the air. If they are buried in a landfill, the chemicals will pollute the soil and groundwater. These damaging materials will remain in the environment for a long time. They can build up in animals' bodies, causing a health risk to the animals themselves and anyone who eats them.

❶ INFORM, an environmental research organization, conducted a study on the best ways to prevent electronic devices from creating poisonous pollution for future generations. ❷ They suggest that manufacturers reduce the poisonous materials used in these devices and come up with sustainable designs which make their reuse easy and economical. ❸ INFORM also asks governments around the world to pass laws encouraging electronics manufacturers to make sustainable designs. ❹ Australia, Japan, the United States, and the European Union are beginning to pass such laws, but even so, it will be years before electronic products can be considered truly environment-friendly.

What we can do to help protect the environment now is to discard our old cellphones safely. Donate your old cellphone to a charity, send it to a group that recycles it, or ask the manufacturer to recondition and resell it. Just don't toss it in the trash!

1. What is the passage mainly about?

   (A) The pollution all over the world.

   (B) The pollution caused by certain chemicals released from cellphones.

   (C) The manufacturing process of cellphones.

   (D) The ban on the use of cellphones in some countries.

2. According to the passage, why used cellphones may endanger our lives?

   (A) People couldn't find a place to burn them.

   (B) There are not enough landfills to bury them.

   (C) They contain some toxic materials.

   (D) INFORM throws them into the groundwater.

3. Which of the following diseases is **NOT** connected to dangerous chemicals based on the passage?

   (A) Nervous system problems.   (B) Flu.

   (C) Reproductive disorders.   (D) Cancer.

4. Which of the following statements is **NOT** a way to prevent old cellphones from creating toxic pollution?

   (A) Tossing used cellphones in the trash.

   (B) Making cellphones easily reusable.

   (C) Passing laws to encourage manufacturers to make sustainable products.

   (D) Donating old cellphones to charities.

5. The sentences in paragraph 3 are numbered ❶ to ❹. Which sentence best indicates what INFORM is? Write down the **NUMBER** of the sentence on the answer sheet.

環境保育

The Magical Amazon River

Though not the world's longest river, the Amazon River forms the world's largest river system that flows through the Amazon basin. The river covers approximately 20 percent of all the water worldwide that pours into the oceans. It is also one of the main habitats for the boto, also known as the Amazon River dolphin, and the notorious piranha.

❶ The Amazon River is also the life force of the Amazon rainforest that covers over a billion acres in Brazil, Venezuela, Columbia, Ecuador, and Peru. ❷ The Amazon rainforest is the home of many surprising species, including the world's largest snakes and freshwater fish. ❸ It also has been described as the "Lungs of the Planet" because it provides the essential environment for converting carbon dioxide into oxygen. ❹ Roughly 5 percent of the world's carbon dioxide is absorbed by the rainforest. ❺ The number might seem small, but the impact is enormous. ❻ Unfortunately, the number is declining.

Despite the growing international concern for environmental protection, the Amazon rainforest is being destroyed every single minute for the profits **it** yields. Over the past 50 years, about 17 percent of the rainforest has been destroyed, which leads to tragic consequences for countries all over the world.

Environmentalists around the world are taking intense actions to save the unique forest before it is too late. Most people are also aware of the need to protect the remaining forest, while at the same time maintaining the lives of the people who depend on them. If managed properly, the rainforest can continuously provide resources for many of the world's needs.

1. The sentences in paragraph 2 are numbered ❶ to ❻. Which sentence best indicates the countries that the Amazon rainforest covers? Write down the **NUMBER** of the sentence on the answer sheet.

2. Which of the following statements is the reason the Amazon rainforest is known as the "Lungs of the Planet"?

   (A) It is located in the center of the planet.

   (B) It is where a massive amount of carbon dioxide is turned into oxygen.

   (C) Notorious piranhas live there.

   (D) It is the main habitat for the Amazon River dolphin.

3. What does the word "**it**" in the third paragraph refer to?

   (A) The profit.   (B) The Amazon River dolphin.

   (C) The problem.   (D) The Amazon rainforest.

4. According to the passage, what caused the mass destruction of the rainforest?

   (A) Economy.   (B) Climate change.

   (C) War.   (D) Insect pests.

5. According to the passage, which of the following statements is **NOT** true?

   (A) The Amazon basin is the world's largest river system.

   (B) About 17 percent of the rainforest has been destroyed.

   (C) The Amazon rainforest houses the world's largest snakes and freshwater fish.

   (D) Forest resources are renewable, so they should be consumed as quickly as possible.

The Cause of Floods and Droughts

Floods are among the world's most serious natural disasters in terms of economic losses and human deaths. Droughts are even worse. **They** can last for decades and result in even greater economic suffering and loss of human lives. Floods and droughts seem to have very different causes: too much water in the case of floods, and too little in the case of droughts. In fact, though, the origin of these disasters is often the same.

❶ Environmentalists agree that man's poor use of the land often increases the chance of droughts and floods. ❷ For example, slash-and-burn agriculture seriously degrades the land. ❸ It is a farming method where the forest is cut and burned down to grow crops. ❹ With the loss of trees and other native plants, the nutrients in the soil will be washed away. ❺ Worse, people often compact the soil for construction, causing it to firm up and become difficult for water to penetrate; also, concrete floors are not able to absorb valuable water. ❻ As a result, during extended dry times, the land dries out, crops wither and die. ❼ Even when a storm brings heavy rainfall, the parched land can no longer take in the water well enough. ❽ The rivers and lakes will overflow and flood the barren earth.

While nature is the force behind heavy rainfalls or extended dry periods, humans and our actions are often the cause of floods and droughts. It seems that water and land management is essential if we are determined to prevent the occurrence of floods and droughts.

1. What does the word "**They**" in the first paragraph refer to?

(A) Droughts.   (B) Economic losses.

(C) Human deaths.   (D) Causes.

2. According to the passage, which of the following is true about droughts?

(A) They can last for a year.

(B) They cause much more damage than floods.

(C) They are usually caused by heavy rainfall.

(D) They will only cause the loss of human life.

3. Which of the following television shows does this passage most likely appear?

(A) A business television show.   (B) A financial television show.

(C) A geographic television show.   (D) A travel television show.

4. The sentences in paragraph 2 are numbered ❶ to ❽. Which sentence best indicates what slash-and-burn agriculture is? Write down the **NUMBER** of the sentence on the answer sheet.

---

5. Which of the following statements is **NOT** supported by the passage?

(A) Human errors are to blame for floods and droughts.

(B) Droughts sometimes remain for years.

(C) Slash-and-burn farming degrades the land, but we can make it rich again by growing crops on it.

(D) Good water and land management is important in protecting the land.

環境保育

73

A Supermoon in the Sky

❶ Have you ever looked into the night sky and thought that the moon looked abnormally large? ❷ If so, you may have seen a supermoon. ❸ Supermoons occur when the moon is at its closest distance to the Earth in its orbit around. ❹ At this time, the moon will be vivid and bright, appearing up to 14 percent larger than usual. ❺ Supermoons happen about once every year, so it's not so often that people have a chance to see them.

Some people believe that supermoons can cause earthquakes and tsunamis. In fact, two major natural disasters in 2004 and 2011 both happened within a two-week period of a supermoon. However, scientists have not found any direct links between supermoons and earthquakes, and they have little effect on tides as well.

In 2015, people celebrating the Chinese Moon Festival experienced a special treat. On the 27th and 28th of September, a supermoon took place during a total lunar eclipse. This made the moon a super blood moon, which was highly visible in the night sky. To promote the event, an airline company in China offered hundreds of special flights that enabled people to see the super blood moon a bit closer. The airline wanted to bring some joy to people traveling during the festival. Those who couldn't share mooncakes with their family could at least see this special moon and be reminded of the holiday.

A blood moon has only happened 5 times since 1900. Anyone who missed this super blood moon will have to wait to see the next one. This incredible lunar event won't happen again until 2033.

1. How does the author begin the passage?

   (A) By giving a definition. (B) By mentioning a story.

   (C) By telling a joke. (D) By comparing two events.

2. The sentences in paragraph 1 are numbered ❶ to ❺. Which sentence best indicates how a "supermoon" takes place? Write down the **NUMBER** of the sentence on the answer sheet.

   _____

3. What can be inferred from the passage?

   (A) Some airlines canceled their flights when supermoons happen.

   (B) Some people believe supermoons are unlucky.

   (C) A total lunar eclipse occurs once a decade.

   (D) Chinese people usually pray to the super blood moon for good luck.

4. Which of the following is **NOT** true about the supermoon?

   (A) A supermoon looks larger than a usual moon.

   (B) Scientists have proved the connection between a supermoon and the occurrence of natural disasters.

   (C) It happens about once every year.

   (D) It appeared in the Chinese Mid-Autumn Festival in 2015.

5. According to the passage, when does a super blood moon happen?

   (A) It happens when the moon is fourteen percent larger than usual.

   (B) It happens when the moon is at its farthest distance to the sun.

   (C) It happens when the tides are the highest.

   (D) It happens when there is a total eclipse of the supermoon.

Noise Pollution No More!

❶ We live in a world that is full of all sorts of sounds. **❷** However, when sounds are unwanted or unpleasant, or if they make us uncomfortable, they can be referred to as "noise pollution." **❸** Noise pollution can interfere with our normal everyday activities, and it can make a person's quality of life worse. **❹** Although some people believe that noise pollution is not as serious as other types of pollution, such as water, air, or land pollution, it is still something that we should pay attention to and do our best to make every effort to prevent or reduce. **❺** In fact, there are several things that governments and people can do to address the problem of noise pollution.

For example, the government should pass laws that make it mandatory for factories and manufacturing to install materials to prevent sound from spreading, especially if **they** have noisy machines. In addition, factories should not be permitted in residential areas. As for transportation terminals, such as airports and bus and train stations, which often produce a lot of noise, the government can ban the use of noisy horns by cars or scooters. Noisy motorbikes and trucks can also be banned from the roads. Apart from that, trees and other bushes should be planted alongside roads and in residential areas since they are useful in absorbing sounds.

At the same time, there are also several things that we can do on our own to combat noise pollution. One easy way is to switch smartphones to silent mode in public places. Rugs, curtains, or even a large bookshelf can also block unwanted noise at home. Finally, if worse comes to worst, you can always buy a pair of earplugs or noise-canceling earphones to come in handy to fight back against noise pollution.

We should do our best to get rid of all types of pollution. However, when it comes to noise pollution, we are fortunate to have a few simple steps that we can all take to prevent or reduce it.

1. The sentences in paragraph 1 are numbered ❶ to ❺. Which sentence best indicates what "noise pollution" is? Write down the **NUMBER** of the sentence on the answer sheet.

_____

2. What does "**they**" in the second paragraph refer to?
   (A) Cars.   (B) Laws.
   (C) Factories.   (D) Transportation terminals.

3. Which of the following items are helpful in combating noise pollution? Please check (✓) all the appropriate boxes.
   ☐ Trees.
   ☐ Rugs.
   ☐ Large bookshelves.
   ☐ Horns.

4. According to the passage, which of the following is **NOT** mentioned as things that the government can do to reduce noise pollution?
   (A) It can ban noisy motorbikes and trucks from the roads.
   (B) It can encourage people to live in the countryside instead of the city.
   (C) It can ban the use of noisy horns by cars or scooters.
   (D) It can pass laws to have factories install soundproofing materials.

5. What is the purpose of the third paragraph?
   (A) To introduce the impact of noise pollution on people's health.
   (B) To explain how government can help reduce noise pollution.
   (C) To give examples of what individuals can do to fight back noise pollution.
   (D) To compare the effect of different items that can prevent sound from spreading.

環境保育

77

You Can Lead a Zero Waste Lifestyle, Too

❶ Plastic packaging and disposable tableware are destroying our environment. ❷ Every time we throw away a paper cup or napkin, and every time we use a plastic fork and knife, we are creating a problem. ❸ Nowadays, a growing number of people are changing their habits and adopting a "zero waste lifestyle" where they try not to create any trash at all. ❹ Here are some things you can do to reduce trash and save our planet.

- **Modify your eating habits:** Use reusable tableware and bring your own knives and forks to restaurants that tend to use paper and plastic containers. You should also remember to ask for a mug, or a glass instead of a paper cup when you go to a coffee shop.

- **Make sure you have eco-friendly household products:** Try replacing paper towels with cloth rags. This way, you will stop filling up landfills with unnecessary trash.

- **Always carry your own shopping bag:** Plastic bags take up to 1,000 years to decompose and are very harmful to the environment.

- **If it's not eco-friendly, don't buy it:** You can convince producers not to sell plastic-wrapped fruit and vegetables if you refuse to buy them. Your purchasing choices can have a large influence on how supermarkets package their goods.

Finally, don't try to do it on your own. **Bring your friends on board!** If you make small changes as a group, you'll stay motivated. Even the smallest change of habits can make our planet a cleaner place.

1. What is the passage mainly about?

   (A) Bringing your own bags to save money.

   (B) Creating an eco-friendly supermarket.

   (C) Saving the planet by reducing the unnecessary trash.

   (D) Lending a helping hand to renewable energy.

2. The sentences in paragraph 1 are numbered ❶ to ❹. Which sentence best describes the definition of "zero waste lifestyle"? Write down the **NUMBER** of the sentence on the answer sheet.

   _____

3. What does "**Bring your friends on board!**" mean in the last paragraph?

   (A) Inviting your friends to lead a trash free life as well.

   (B) Asking your friends to buy you wrapped fruit.

   (C) Bringing your friends to go on an adventurous trip with you.

   (D) Making your friends support your decision not to use paper cups.

4. Which of the following statements is true?

   (A) The government should have more landfills specifically for plastic bags.

   (B) Paper towels cost more than cloth rags.

   (C) People like to use disposable tableware because it is cleaner.

   (D) Small changes in our lives can make a big difference to the planet.

5. According to the passage, which of the following is **NOT** mentioned as a way to reduce trash?

   (A) Use a mug rather than a paper cup at the coffee shop.

   (B) Carry personal shopping bags.

   (C) Turn off the light when leaving a room.

   (D) Bring personal chopsticks and spoons to restaurants.

Preserving Natural Areas

Protecting natural areas is a challenge. Although people enjoy spending time there, they leave their marks wherever they go: waste, garbage, pollution, and other kinds of damage to wildlife. Often, this damage is accidental, but even something as simple as taking a walk can have a big impact because every footstep runs the risk of destroying something beautiful.

One way to protect nature is to establish national parks and other protected areas where visitors require permission before entering. **This** allows the people who manage the areas to control the number of visitors at any given time, which decreases the amount of damage that visitors cause. Charging an entrance fee also helps to cover the costs of looking after the park and of supporting conservation efforts.

❶ Another way to protect natural areas is to put limits on what activities people can do there. ❷ For example, motorboats are not allowed in some lakes because they may cause pollution and unwelcome noise. ❸ Many parks don't allow people to build fires—a human activity that often leads to wildfires every year. ❹ Similarly, many waterfront areas are protected against industrial development, and many forests are off-limits to loggers.

Such laws and rules are fine, but they won't work unless people follow them. Education is desperately needed. People who head for the wilderness need to be made aware of how easily the natural environment can be damaged. This education must start early, and responsibility for it lies within parents, teachers, and governments. Only if people learn to appreciate what they have will they make the decision to protect it.

1. What does "**This**" in the second paragraph refer to?

   (A) Establishing national parks and other protected areas.

   (B) Taking a walk in natural areas.

   (C) Charging an entrance fee.

   (D) Putting a limit on motorboats.

2. Which of the following is **NOT** true about national parks?

   (A) Visitors will need permission to get in.

   (B) The entrance fee can cover the costs of looking after the places.

   (C) It is easier for the people who manage the areas to keep the number of visitors under control.

   (D) Visitors are likely to do more damage to the nature in these parks.

3. Where does this passage most likely appear?

   (A) A beauty magazine.   (B) A motorboat catalog.

   (C) A national park brochure.   (D) An article on survival skills.

4. The sentences in paragraph 3 are numbered ❶ to ❹. Which sentence best indicates the reason why motorboats are not allowed in some lakes? Write down the **NUMBER** of the sentence on the answer sheet.

5. What can be inferred from the passage?

   (A) The government won't pass any law to protect natural areas unless its people want it to do so.

   (B) The industrial development of waterfront areas is beneficial to economic growth.

   (C) Human activities can sometimes cause great damage to natural areas.

   (D) People can enter protected areas whenever they like.

The Rise of the Superweeds

Two decades ago, American farming companies introduced new kinds of crops to boost harvests. They altered the genes of major crops like soybeans, cotton, corn, and sugar cane. These special crops were designed to resist the powerful chemical poisons that the companies also developed to kill weeds. The companies believed they had started a revolution in agriculture that could benefit farmers and consumers for centuries. Weeds would no longer choke the growth of crops on these huge farms. It seemed that mankind had conquered nature and won a victory over weeds.

❶ However, some disturbing phenomena began to be observed on farmland growing these weed-free crops. ❷ By interfering with nature in this way, it appeared the farmers had actually started a natural process in the weeds. ❸ Some surviving weeds were found to have naturally-occurring genes that allowed them to resist the poisons. ❹ These plants bred, and soon many species of such weeds became resistant to the chemicals.

The situation is very alarming nowadays. It's said that over ninety percent of the cotton and soybean fields in the southeastern United States have lost control of the spread of these tough superweeds. The companies have to spend more money on removing the weeds with machines or by hiring workers. Therefore the land is becoming less productive and less profitable. Many farms are using more powerful poisons to kill the weeds, but this will continue to create weeds that develop resistance to the chemicals. Moreover, these chemicals have been linked to cancer among farm workers, and the wind also carries the poisons to local populations.

The rise of the superweeds seems to indicate that farming companies using these methods are fighting a losing battle against an old enemy.

1. According to the passage, which of the following crops is **NOT** severely affected because of superweeds?

   (A) Corn. (B) Sugar cane. (C) Cotton. (D) Banana.

2. Which of the following can be inferred from the passage?

   (A) Since the introduction of weed-free crops, the cotton yields in the United States has been triple.

   (B) The genes of weeds are gradually modified due to the introduction of weed-free crops.

   (C) The chemicals farming companies used have little impact on human health.

   (D) Farming companies have successfully found a way to keep superweeds under control.

3. The sentences in paragraph 2 are numbered ❶ to ❹. Which sentence best describes the main feature of superweeds? Write down the **NUMBER** of the sentence on the answer sheet.

   環境保育

4. Which of the following is **NOT** a measure taken by farming companies and farmers to deal with superweeds?

   (A) Using more powerful chemicals to kill them.

   (B) Hiring workers to get rid of them.

   (C) Setting fields on fire and burn them to ashes.

   (D) Using machines to remove them.

5. Which of the following best describes the author's attitude towards those farming companies trying to eliminate superweeds with chemicals?

   (A) Pessimistic. (B) Optimistic. (C) Uplifted. (D) Conservative.

Climate Change and Our Mental Health

Climate change is a popular topic these days. Our planet's temperature is rising, causing chain reactions. The polar ice caps are melting, and rising sea levels will leave many coastal cities underwater.

❶ In the coming decades, as our climate changes, life on our planet will be very different. ❷ All the scientific theories suggest that life will become harder. ❸ Moreover, social scientists think that our planet will become more conflict-ridden due to limited resources. ❹ Not only is our physical well-being under risk, our mental health is also in danger. ❺ Because of climate change, many young people are extremely worried and concerned about a future full of floods, pollution, and food shortages. ❻ Some psychologists call this "eco-anxiety." ❼ People with this condition are very pessimistic about the future, and their negative thoughts often prevent them from being happy.

We're all aware that future generations will have to deal with extreme weather conditions. It is also obvious that in the future, mental health problems like eco-anxiety will be on the rise. To reduce anxiety about the future, psychologists suggest that we should take actions to deal with the problems rather than get too worried. Becoming an environmental activist, staying informed about environmental issues, and educating others will also make you a person who **has both feet on the ground**.

1. Which of the following is **NOT** mentioned as a chain reaction caused by climate change?
   (A) Rising sea levels.　　　　(B) More environmental activists.
   (C) Floods.　　　　(D) Underwater cities.

2. The sentences in paragraph 2 are numbered ❶ to ❼. Which sentence best describes the concern many young people have due to climate change? Write down the **NUMBER** of the sentence on the answer sheet.

   _____

3. What is the second paragraph mainly about?
   (A) It gives examples of how extreme weather conditions affected people's lives in different countries.
   (B) It demonstrates how people can help to fight against climate change.
   (C) It lists the problems that climate refugees caused around the world.
   (D) It explains how climate change influences people's mental health.

4. What does the phrase "**has both feet on the ground**" in the third paragraph most likely mean?
   (A) To keep away from flooding areas. (B) To take actions on one's own.
   (C) To become friendly.　　　　(D) To become active and practical.

5. Where does this passage most likely appear?
   (A) A geography magazine.　　　　(B) A fashion magazine.
   (C) An interior design magazine.　　　　(D) A digital camera magazine.

85

Unit 40

Fighting Food Waste

❶ You might not be aware of it, but food waste is a global problem. **❷** Every year, millions of tons of food go to the trash, before they even get to the table. **❸** As customers, we want our food to look attractive. **❹** Therefore, we throw out food that is fresh enough to eat but not good-looking. **❺** The entire food production chain does this. **❻** As for producers, they tend to throw away ugly fruit and vegetables because shipping items that might go unsold would cost more than throwing them away. **❼** Then the entire food supply chain, supermarkets, restaurants **repeat the same behavior**.

The good news is that many companies around the world are fighting food waste. UK-based app "Olio," for example, collects a considerable amount of food that restaurants and individuals no longer want or need every day. The food is still fresh enough to eat. Users of the app can collect unwanted food for free. That way, food goes to the people who appreciate it rather than goes to the trash.

On the other side of the world, a Canadian charity "Second Harvest" has created a supermarket where all the food is free. The supermarket looks like any other grocery store with fresh food. However, it is filled with food donated from supermarkets because they throw away food that isn't sold within a few days.

In conclusion, millions of people are hungry, yet there is still food waste. This might disturb you, but it's a sad reality. Moreover, this behavior is harmful for the environment. We put so much effort in producing food, only to throw away tons of it. Food waste is a global problem, but many people are working to fight against it and find effective solutions.

1. The sentences in paragraph 1 are numbered ❶ to ❼. Which sentence best explains why producers throw away ugly fruit? Write down the **NUMBER** of the sentence on the answer sheet.

_____

2. What does "**repeat the same behavior**" mean in the first paragraph?

   (A) Sell unwanted food at a low price.

   (B) Throw away ugly fruit and vegetables.

   (C) Give away food no longer needed to the poor.

   (D) Ship unsold food to Third World countries.

3. Which of the following is **NOT** true about the app Olio?

   (A) It is a UK-based app.

   (B) It collects fresh but unwanted food from restaurants and individuals.

   (C) It helps unwanted food go to those who need it.

   (D) It allows its users to work on farms to exchange for free food.

4. How is this passage organized?

   (A) By comparison and contrast.

   (B) In the sequence of time.

   (C) By stating problems and solutions.

   (D) By cause and effect.

5. What can we infer from the passage?

   (A) The founder of Second Harvest cares about the issue of food waste.

   (B) Wasting food does no harm to the environment.

   (C) Customers' preference has nothing to do with food waste.

   (D) Many supermarkets refuse to work with Second Harvest because they consider its supermarket a competitor.

87

Globesity

❶ The new word "globesity," which is short for "global obesity," describes the world's fastest-growing health problem. ❷ According to the World Health Organization (WHO), globesity has nearly tripled since 1975; over 650 million people have been overweight by far. ❸ These people have higher chances of developing diabetes, heart disease, and some cancers. ❹ The International Obesity Task Force is asking world leaders to help spread the message that people must eat more fiber, but less sugar and fat. ❺ Moreover, getting adequate exercise is also necessary.

Many experts blame the world's weight problem on changing lifestyles. Research also says that 60 percent of weight gained is due to lack of exercise. More and more people tend to work long hours in the office. We take a car, bus, or train to work instead of walking or biking. At the end of the day, we return home too tired to prepare a healthy meal, so we grab fast food or convenience food high in fat, salt, and sugar instead. After eating, we spend the rest of the evening sitting on the couch watching television. With this routine, it's hard to imagine what a healthy lifestyle is.

So, what is the solution? Experts suggest that people should eat wholegrain foods, fresh fruit and vegetables because they help digestion. Nuts, as well as lean meat are also essential to our bodies because they provide good fat and protein. And, of course, we need to get more exercise. A 20-minute walk each day can help us become healthier.

1. The sentences in paragraph 1 are numbered 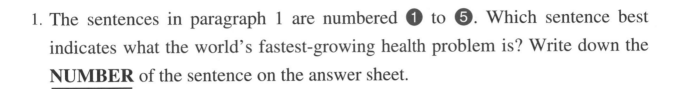 ❶ to ❺. Which sentence best indicates what the world's fastest-growing health problem is? Write down the **NUMBER** of the sentence on the answer sheet.

_____

2. According to the passage, which of the following is **NOT** mentioned as a disease that overweight people are more likely to get?

   (A) Diabetes.　　(B) Insomnia.　　(C) Heart disease.　(D) Cancer.

3. How does the author begin the passage?

   (A) By providing statistics.

   (B) By mentioning an international sports event.

   (C) By giving a definition.

   (D) By comparing different people's reactions.

4. Which of the following statements is **NOT** true about obesity?

   (A) Obesity makes people too tired to prepare a healthy meal.

   (B) Obesity is one of the most important public health problems.

   (C) Weight gain often results from lack of exercise.

   (D) Eating more fresh fruit and vegetables might make people healthier.

5. What can be inferred from the passage?

   (A) Obesity is a disease that cannot be cured.

   (B) Obesity is related to the way people live.

   (C) 50 percent of the world's population is overweight.

   (D) In the last few decades, obesity has grown by 60 percent.

醫學保健

Unit 42

Small Puff, Big Problem

Smoking is the leading risk factor for lung cancer. Tobacco smoke contains thousands of chemical substances, more than 60 substances of which are known to cause cancer. People usually associate smoking with males, thinking men account for the majority of deaths from lung cancer. Yet, recent reports have shown that the number of smoking females increases rapidly, and women have a higher chance of getting lung cancer than men.

Research shows that tobacco affects genders differently. Compared with men, women are more likely to develop lung cancer at a younger age when they are exposed to tobacco smoke at the same level as men. According to statistics, lung cancer kills more women every year than breast cancer, and 20 percent of female cancer patients are non-smokers! Women are also more likely to develop small-cell lung cancer, which spreads quickly. Estrogen (a female hormone) is also thought to play a key role in stimulating the growth of lung cancer cells. Even though smoking is harmful, one out of every five women in the U.S. still smokes. These women do not comprehend the degree of the risk that they are taking while smoking.

❶ Although medical treatments keep improving, the 5-year survival rate for people with lung cancer is only 19 percent. ❷ The best way to prevent lung cancer is simply to quit (or better never to start) smoking. ❸ The risk for lung cancer increases with the quantity, duration, and intensity of smoking. ❹ Women who stop smoking greatly reduce their risk of dying prematurely, so quitting smoking is beneficial at all ages.

Recently, people all over the world have started to pay more attention to the problem of smoking among women. Aggressive campaigns have been launched against tobacco companies. We must act to draw the public's attention to the impact of smoking on women's health and counter the tobacco industry's strategies targeting at women to help in the anti-cancer battle.

1. What is the passage mainly about?

   (A) Women's smoking and the health problems it causes.

   (B) The relation between smoking and breast cancer.

   (C) How young women try to quit smoking.

   (D) How tobacco companies encourage young women to smoke.

2. According to the passage, what percentage of women in the U.S. smoke?

   (A) 12–15 percent. (B) 60 percent.　　(C) 90 percent.　　(D) 20 percent.

3. Which of the following is **NOT** supported by the passage?

   (A) The number of women dying of breast cancer is higher than that of women dying of lung cancer.

   (B) A female hormone makes women more likely to have lung cancer than men.

   (C) Less than 20 percent of lung-cancer patients can be cured with modern treatments.

   (D) Activists around the world are working hard to stop tobacco companies' strategies targeting at female consumers.

4. Where does this passage most likely be found?

   (A) In a history book.　　　　　　(B) In a medical report.

   (C) In a fashion magazine.　　　　(D) In a political science journal.

5. The sentences in paragraph 3 are numbered ❶ to ❹. Which sentence best indicates the best way to prevent lung cancer? Write down the **NUMBER** of the sentence on the answer sheet.

醫學保健

91

Unit 43

Pain in the Back

You are not alone if you have back pain. It is one of the most frequent complaints among people. **It goes beyond age, economy, or race.** Almost 80 percent of the population worldwide will encounter or has encountered some forms of back pain during the lifetime. In our society, back pain has become a universal illness and the main reason why people seek medical treatment.

❶ There are many causes of back pain. ❷ Muscle strain or spasm caused by heavy physical work, awkward bending or twisting, poor posture could add up to serious back pain. ❸ In general, inactive jobs and the lifestyle of people have become a major cause of back pain today. ❹ The physical symptoms of this illness can range from a dull, annoying ache to absolute suffering, and may lead to ineffectiveness at work and even disabilities. ❺ In the United States, back-pain patients spend over US$ 100 billion every year for medical examination and treatment.

Proper rest combined with appropriate exercise and medication is often the primary method of therapy if the pain is mild. An ice bag or hot-water bottle applied to the back may also help to ease the pain. In most cases, surgery is not required for the treatment of back pain. Often acute back pain goes away by itself in a few days or weeks. Yet, if the pain lasts for some time despite these handy methods, surgery might be the most efficient solution.

Whether you will have back pain or not depends on how you use your back, both at work and at home. If you want to keep your back healthy, it is important to keep it moving. Even if you are staying still, you should support the back well. In addition, use proper posture, start a persistent home exercise program, and maintain a sensible diet for a healthy body weight to keep back pain away.

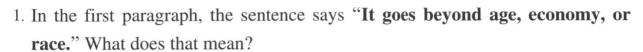

1. In the first paragraph, the sentence says "**It goes beyond age, economy, or race.**" What does that mean?

   (A) Age, economic or ethnic barriers are the main reasons for back pain.

   (B) Anyone might suffer from back pain regardless of ages, economic conditions, or ethnic origins.

   (C) Back pain only hurts those with age, economic, or ethnic barriers.

   (D) People with back pain do not recognize age, economic, or ethnic barriers.

2. Which of the following is **NOT** listed in the passage as a cause of back pain?

   (A) Awkward bending or twisting.　　(B) Poor posture.

   (C) Heavy physical work.　　　　　　(D) A sensible diet.

3. The sentences in paragraph 2 are numbered ❶ to ❺. Which sentence best indicates how much money back-pain patients in the U.S. spend on medical examination and treatment every year? Write down the **NUMBER** of the sentence on the answer sheet.

   _____

4. Which of the following statements is true about back pain?

   (A) Most of back-pain patients need surgery.

   (B) Most of the population will not have back pain.

   (C) Back pain will often disappear by itself.

   (D) Back pain will not be relieved without a surgery.

5. Which of the following statement is ture?

   (A) Consistent home exercise can keep back pain away.

   (B) Only people who have certain jobs suffer from back pain.

   (C) Putting an ice bag on the back cannot help ease the pain.

   (D) Back pain is a worldwide phenomenon but will never lead to disabilities.

Sugar or Not?

❶ Research tells us that babies are born with a preference for sweetness over other tastes. ❷ For many of us, this preference continues for the rest of our lives. ❸ However, sweet foods in our diets can be, more or less, harmful to our bodies. ❹ Apart from spoiling your appetite and decaying teeth, sugar also makes it difficult to control our weight. ❺ People have tried to eat few sweet foods, but it is hard to completely give up sweets. ❻ If we want to enjoy sweet-tasting foods without sugar, sugar substitutes are one option. ❼ However, there are some concerns about sugar substitutes that might make us wonder if these ingredients are good for our bodies.

One frequent concern about sugar substitutes is their safety issue. "Saccharin" and "aspartame" are two of the most common sugar substitutes. They can be found in products such as chewing gum and ice cream. Critics have been questioning these artificial chemicals since studies linked saccharin to cancer according to lab experiments. On the other hand, supporters, especially diabetes patients who need to reduce sugar consumption, claim **they** are not dangerous in a small amount. Although there is no certainty that these substances can cause cancer in humans, we can't be too careful when it comes to eating something that is not natural.

The second concern about sugar substitutes is that some people believe artificial sweeteners can help people lose weight because most of them are low in calories. In fact, there is no reliable evidence indicating that. In other words, they are not magic foods that will melt pounds away; they can only be helpful in an overall weight control program that includes exercise and a healthy diet.

Sugar substitutes will not necessarily put our health in danger, but they won't do us any good, either. If we want to lose weight, strengthening our self-control and cutting excessive sugar out of our diet by choosing healthier foods might be the best way.

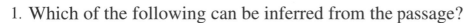

1. Which of the following can be inferred from the passage?

   (A) Babies prefer sweetness over saltiness.

   (B) Sugar helps boost energy.

   (C) Saccharin causes high blood pressure in humans.

   (D) Sugar substitutes are good for our mental health.

2. The sentences in paragraph 1 are numbered ❶ to ❼. Which sentence best indicates the harm that sugar may do to our bodies? Write down the **NUMBER** of the sentence on the answer sheet.

   _____

3. What does the word "**they**" refer to in the second paragraph?

   (A) Critics.   (B) Saccharin and aspartame.

   (C) Supporters.   (D) Chewing gum and ice cream.

4. According to the passage, which of the following is different in meaning from the other three?

   (A) Sugar substitute.   (B) Aspartame.

   (C) Artificial sweetener.   (D) Sweet food.

5. According to the passage, which of the following statements can't help people lose weight?

   (A) Increasing the amount of sugar in one's diet.

   (B) Eating healthy foods.

   (C) Using artificial sweeteners.

   (D) Exercising regularly.

醫學保健

Unit 45

Fighting Fatigue

Fatigue is a condition in which people feel very tired and weary. Most people have experienced fatigue at one time or another, due to lack of sleep or an illness.

Some examples of fatigue-causing conditions are the following: stress, hormone imbalance, depression, heart, lung and blood disease, and cancer. Lack of exercise and poor physical condition can cause fatigue as well. Many jobs are **computer-based** now. People spend more time typing and clicking before a screen. As a result, many people lose muscles and gain fat because they are not burning enough calories. Sometimes, people can suffer from fatigue with no obvious cause, so the most important thing is to get lots of sleep to recharge your body. Next time when your parents try to wake you up on the weekend, you can tell them you need the rest to prevent fatigue!

❶ Aside from getting enough rest, it is also important to follow a balanced diet. ❷ A proper diet is one of the easiest ways to avoid fatigue since our bodies need fuel to carry out important daily functions such as digestion, blood circulation, and waste removal. ❸ Another way to prevent fatigue is to exercise regularly. ❹ Exercise, like weight lifting, walking, and aerobics, can help build muscles and reduce body fat. ❺ More muscles and lower levels of fat make you more energetic.

1. According to the passage, which of the following is **NOT** mentioned as a cause of fatigue?

   (A) Lack of sleep.   (B) Hangover.

   (C) Hormone imbalance.   (D) Heart disease.

2. Why is "**computer-based**" mentioned in the second paragraph?

   (A) To explain how modern people lose muscles and gain fat gradually.

   (B) To give an example about why modern people spend more time indoors.

   (C) To describe the relation between modern people and the Internet.

   (D) To prove how staring at screens for a long time causes damage to human bodies.

3. Which of the following statements is **NOT** true about fatigue?

   (A) Muscle loss may lead to fatigue.

   (B) Following a balanced diet can help you avoid fatigue.

   (C) The reason why fatigue happens can always be found.

   (D) Fatigue may result from a blood disease.

4. According to the passage, what are the ways to avoid fatigue? Please check (✓) all the appropriate boxes.

   ☐ Get more sleep.

   ☐ Take regular exercise.

   ☐ Eat a balanced diet.

   ☐ Work long hours.

5. The sentences in paragraph 3 are numbered ❶ to ❺. Which sentence best indicates the reason why our bodies need a proper diet? Write down the **NUMBER** of the sentence on the answer sheet.

醫學保健

Fever Helps Us Fight Diseases

It seems that we all have a little fever sometimes. Exercising, dancing, eating, getting angry, and even falling in love—all these things make our body temperature rise. These are friendly fevers; we don't have to take a pill. The "real" fever that we all are familiar with, unfortunately, is of a different kind altogether. Nobody enjoys the heat and headaches a "real" fever causes. But maybe it's about time we learned to appreciate fever despite the discomfort it brings.

❶ Our normal temperature should hover near 37°C. ❷ When the temperature of our bodies passes the 37.5°C mark, we might have a fever. ❸ We naturally associate fever with being bed-ridden and having sore joints and chills. ❹ In fact, fever is usually a signal of other sickness. ❺ Anything from an ear infection to cancer could cause our temperature to climb. ❻ This is because whenever bacteria or viruses invade the body, **it** uses heat to kill them off, resulting in the high temperature. ❼ Fever also makes the body's immune system work more productively. ❽ Once body heat rises, more white blood cells and antibodies are released. ❾ Fever is, therefore, a defense mechanism.

What should we do when fever strikes? The best things we can do when fever strikes are to take a warm bath, drink more water, and get a complete rest. Remember: fever is a way that body uses to warn us of the invasion of bacteria and viruses. However, if your condition does not get better, consulting a doctor might be the best solution.

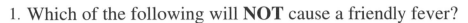

1. Which of the following will **NOT** cause a friendly fever?

   (A) Getting angry.   (B) A lung infection.

   (C) Falling in love.   (D) Exercising.

2. What does "**it**" in the second paragraph refer to?

   (A) Bacteria.   (B) Infection.   (C) Medicine.   (D) Human body.

3. The sentences in paragraph 2 are numbered ❶ to ❾. Which sentence best indicates the body temperature at which we get a fever? Write down the **NUMBER** of the sentence on the answer sheet.

_____

4. Which of the following is true?

   (A) Fever only causes heat and headaches.

   (B) Most cases of fever result from cancer.

   (C) Fever brings discomfort, but it's a defense mechanism.

   (D) Once fever happens, consult a doctor immediately.

5. According to the passage, which of the following statements is **NOT** true?

   (A) Sometimes fever is a signal of sickness.

   (B) Once bacteria or viruses invade the body, white blood cells and antibodies try to kill them.

   (C) A fever makes the body's immune system work better.

   (D) A cancer patient will have lower body temperature than normal.

醫學保健

Unit 47

What Happens when We Become Angry?

We all know how an angry person looks — wide-eyed and red-faced, with hands shaking and veins bulging out in his or her neck and temples. But why does an angry person look this way? To answer this question, we must go back thousands of years to a time in human history when people often faced threats from wild animals, from nature, and from each other. For early humans, feeling angry usually meant there were physical dangers. Scientists refer to these body responses as the fight-or-flight reflex, that is, anger can force our early ancestors to make immediate decisions for survival. Thankfully, for most of us, the physical dangers that made our early ancestors angry have disappeared. But even though the triggers for anger might have changed, the body's responses to anger haven't.

❶ Our bodies produce a kind of natural chemical called adrenaline when we get angry. ❷ It will enter our bloodstream, make us feel excited, sharpen our reflexes, and speed up our reaction. ❸ As this happens, our heart rate increases from resting heart rate of around 80 beats per minute to around 180 beats per minute. ❹ Besides, our blood pressure and body temperature both rise. ❺ Our breathing becomes faster and more shallow. ❻ Our muscles will tense up for action because more blood flows into muscle tissue. ❼ The pupils in our eyes will open wide to let in more light for sharper vision. ❽ Our bodies will burn calories very quickly, causing the shaking that we often see in angry people.

All these years later, the body still equates anger with danger. Our natural body responses haven't changed. Whenever we are angry or under threats, our bodies will still get ready for intense action as our ancestors did.

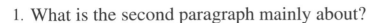

1. What is the second paragraph mainly about?

   (A) Why people get angry.

   (B) How the human body reacts to anger.

   (C) How our ancestors avoided physical dangers.

   (D) What people can do to keep their temper under control.

2. The sentences in paragraph 2 are numbered ❶ to ❽. Which sentence best indicates the chemical which will enter our bloodstream when we get angry? Write down the **NUMBER** of the sentence on the answer sheet.

   _____

3. According to the passage, which of the following is mentioned as a reaction when people get angry?

   (A) Their heartbeat slows down.

   (B) They feel excited and their muscles relax.

   (C) Their blood pressure and body temperature both rise.

   (D) Their reactions slow down.

4. Which of the following statements is **NOT** supported by the passage?

   (A) Our ancestors looked red-faced when they became angry.

   (B) It was common for our ancestors to be attacked by wild animals.

   (C) Our body still associates anger with danger.

   (D) When people get angry, less blood flows into their muscle tissue.

5. According to the passage, what can we infer about people's responses to anger?

   (A) People's responses to anger have disappeared.

   (B) People's responses to anger depend on when and where they live.

   (C) People's responses to anger can make their hearts beat 80 beats per minute.

   (D) People's responses to anger remain the same as those of their ancestors'.

醫學保健

Unit 48

Keeping Our Blood Supplies Safe

If you are ever in a serious accident, you may need a blood transfusion to save your life. It is a medical process where blood is injected into a patient's body to provide the missing components, such as red blood cells or white blood cells. But have you ever worried about the safety of the blood you might receive during a surgery? From now on, you should know more about what has been done to keep our blood supplies safe because it's often a matter of life and death.

International Federation of Red Cross and Red Crescent and other similar organizations across the world work hard to assure a safe supply of blood for medical emergencies. There are three major steps to make sure the blood is clean and available.

❶ The first step is to accept blood only from people who volunteer to give their blood freely—never from paid donors. ❷ Unpaid donors are more likely to answer a series of screening questions truthfully. ❸ The reason is that these people will not donate their blood for money. ❹ There is, therefore, no benefit for them to lie about their health. ❺ Health-related questions such as "What medications are you taking?" and "What practices do you follow to assure you have safe sex?" are the first line of defense against infected blood. ❻ If the volunteers' answers show that they may carry a disease or they don't seem healthy enough to give their blood at the moment, they will be rejected.

Once blood is collected from healthy volunteers, technicians test it for several different diseases, including AIDS, hepatitis, and syphilis. Only the blood that passes all of the lab tests is processed further. Then, the blood is put through a filter to remove its white blood cells, which often cause rejection reactions in transfusion patients.

Finally, after all of these processes, technicians label and store the blood. To make sure it remains safe for use, **they** store it in secure areas until it is needed. Organizations that collect and distribute blood take the safety very seriously. "Our blood supplies are safer than ever," according to the Red Cross. So, if you are ever in a position to need donated blood, you can depend on its safety.

1. What is the purpose of the passage?

   (A) To explain what kind of person can donate blood.

   (B) To encourage us to donate our blood.

   (C) To show us how safe donated blood is.

   (D) To make sure that paid blood donors are strictly screened.

2. The sentences in paragraph 3 are numbered ❶ to ❻. Which sentence best indicates the health-related questions the donor will be asked? Write down the **NUMBER** of the sentence on the answer sheet.

   _____

3. Which of the following is the correct order of processing donated blood?

   (A) Collect blood → test → filter → label and store.

   (B) Collect blood → label and store → filter → test.

   (C) Collect blood → label and store → test → filter.

   (D) Test → collect blood → label and store → filter.

4. Which of the following statements is true based on the passage?

   (A) A filter will help to remove the red blood cells of the blood.

   (B) Everyone will get paid for giving blood.

   (C) Paid donors are more willing to answer some private questions.

   (D) Unhealthy people will be rejected for donating blood.

5. What does "**they**" in the last paragraph refer to?

   (A) Blood supplies. (B) Donors.   (C) Technicians.   (D) Organizations.

醫學保健

103

Should You Be Afraid of Your Food?

Human technology advances at lightning speed, but not always without mistakes. Efforts to improve our production and quality of food have led to great controversy over the safety of food. A new term has been made to describe the public's feelings toward potentially harmful food: food scare.

The term "food scare" originally referred to anxiety over the safety of genetically modified (GM) foods. While selective breeding within the same species has been used for centuries, scientists can now transfer genes from one species to another. For instance, a gene keeping fish from freezing in winter may be put into vegetables so that a farmer can plant seeds earlier in the season for more profit. However, there is little research to indicate the long-term effects of GM foods on human body. What if a gene causing allergies in one food ends up in another, and consumers have severe reactions? Even worse, what if GM foods become poisonous?

❶ Chemicals such as pesticides and insecticides cause concerns. ❷ Chemicals used to keep crops safe from insects and diseases stay on the produce after harvest and are consumed by people and animals. ❸ Some chemicals, like DDT, have been linked to various illnesses and developmental disorders. ❹ The use of added ingredients also causes concern. ❺ They are chemicals added to food to preserve freshness or change the color. ❻ Although they may not cause immediate food poisoning, they have been blamed for allergies, hormone imbalances, digestive problems, and cancer.

To eat safer food, many people have turned to chemical-free and environmentally-friendly organic produce. Also, organizations like the United States Food and Drug Administration (FDA) and the United Kingdom's Food Standards Agency (FSA) are dedicated to improving food labeling to make sure that consumers get enough information about the food they eat. With their efforts, consumers can buy products intelligently. Hopefully, we will one day be free from food scares.

1. What is the passage mainly about?

    (A) How pesticides and insecticides improve human life.

    (B) People's anxiety over what they eat.

    (C) How the authorities fight food poisoning.

    (D) The development of GM food.

2. Which of the following is **NOT** mentioned as a part of people's food scare in the passage?

    (A) People are worried about the effects GM foods might have on human body.

    (B) Added ingredients may cause various allergies.

    (C) Chemicals remain in the produce after harvest.

    (D) People are madly drawn to sugary snacks and drinks due to additives.

3. Which of the following best describe the author's attitude towards GM foods?

    (A) Doubtful.　　(B) Positive.　　(C) Despised.　　(D) Pleased.

4. The sentences in paragraph 3 are numbered ❶ to ❻. Which sentence best indicates the problems that food additives can cause to human bodies? Write down the **NUMBER** of the sentence on the answer sheet.

_____

5. According to the passage, which of the following statements is **NOT** true?

    (A) Advanced technology is not always good for us.

    (B) People are concerned about the safety of GM food.

    (C) A lot of people prefer chemical-free organic produce.

    (D) The United States FDA guarantees that GM foods are without added ingredients.

醫學保健

Too Busy to Be Healthy

Most people know that they aren't getting as much exercise as they need, but they keep telling themselves, "Next week I'm going to start getting in shape." Of course next week is really busy, and they postpone it until the next. And the next. The truth is, our modern life is very busy, and it's difficult for us to find the time to stay fit.

This is a relatively modern problem, because years ago, physical fitness was a part of life. People walked to school or to work, or rode their bikes, often for long distances. Also, many farmers worked the land, exercising their muscles for a long time in the sun and fresh air. These time-consuming chores were part of life. The descendants of these fit laborers, however, probably work in an office, sitting at a desk all day long. For lunch, they are too busy to eat a healthy meal. Then, after work, they walk to their cars, drive home and sit in front of the TV until they go to sleep. This inactive, high-fat lifestyle has led to increasing obesity, heart disease, and occasionally a shorter life.

❶ So, what can people do about this health crisis? ❷ For one thing, people can start riding their bikes or walking instead of driving on short trips. ❸ For another, people can get up regularly from their desks and stretch. ❹ According to research, thirty minutes of vigorous activity every day is all that is needed to stay fit. ❺ "Always take the stairs and never the elevator," said a Japanese trainer of Olympians when asked how to stay in shape. ❻ You could also take a walk around the neighborhood after work, and urge your children to engage in real sports instead of video games. ❼ Every little change you make will finally pay off in a healthier body and perhaps a longer life.

1. What is the main purpose of this passage?

   (A) To show us how people go to work.

   (B) To emphasize how busy the lifestyle of modern people is.

   (C) To state the importance of exercising.

   (D) To depict the place where young people eat.

2. According to the passage, which of the following is **NOT** caused by an inactive high-fat lifestyle?

   (A) Obesity.   (B) Dying earlier.   (C) Heart disease.   (D) Starvation.

3. According to the passage, which of the following is **NOT** a way to help us stay fit?

   (A) To walk to work.

   (B) To take the stairs.

   (C) To walk to the car, and drive home.

   (D) To take a walk around the neighborhood.

4. The sentences in paragraph 3 are numbered ❶ to ❼. Which sentence best indicates the amount of time that people need to exercisc to stay fit? Write down the **NUMBER** of the sentence on the answer sheet.

   _____

5. According to the passage, which of the following statements is **NOT** true?

   (A) Modern life is very busy, and it's hard to find time to exercise.

   (B) A Japanese trainer of Olympians exercises thirty minutes every day to stay fit.

   (C) Years ago, physical fitness was part of people's everyday life.

   (D) It might be hard to keep fit if you work in an office, sitting at a desk all day.

醫學保健

107

透過閱讀，你我得以跨越時空，一窺那已無法觸及的世界。

閱讀經典文學時光之旅：英國篇

宋美璍／編著

閱讀經典文學時光之旅：美國篇

陳彰範／編著

★ 各書精選8篇經典英美文學作品，囊括各類議題，如性別平等、人權、海洋教育等。帶你在閱讀過後，能領略作者的所思所慮，以及所處時代的價值觀。

★ 獨家收錄故事背景的知識補充。

★ 附精闢賞析、文章中譯及電子朗讀音檔，自學也能輕鬆讀懂文學作品。

★ 可搭配新課綱加深加廣選修課程及多元選修課程。

第一本中文詳解圖形組織圖 (G.O.) 的英文閱讀書！

英文閱讀G.O., G.O., G.O.!

應惠蕙／編著
Peter John Wilds／審訂

Graphic Organizers for Effective Reading!

★ 精選18種實用圖形組織圖，最常用的G.O.通通有！

★ 全書共12課，多元文體搭配12種圖形組織圖，閱讀素材通通有！

★ 每課搭配G.O.練習題與4題閱讀測驗，組織架構、閱讀練習通通有！

★ 閱讀測驗加入最新大考題型──圖片題，準備大考通通有！

★ 隨書附贈翻譯與解析本，中譯詳解通通有！

★ 學校團訂贈送6回隨堂評量卷，單字測驗、翻譯練習通通有！

★ 隨書附贈朗讀音檔，雲端下載，隨載隨聽！

國家圖書館出版品預行編目資料

Intermediate Reading：英文閱讀High Five／王隆興編
著.——初版二刷.——臺北市：三民，2022
　　面；　　公分.——（Reading Power系列）

　ISBN 978−957−14−6835−8　（平裝）
　1. 英語 2. 詞彙

805.12　　　　　　　　　　　　　　　　109007635

 Reading Power 系列

Intermediate Reading：英文閱讀 High Five

編 著 者	王隆興
發 行 人	劉振強
出 版 者	三民書局股份有限公司
地　　址	臺北市復興北路 386 號 (復北門市)
	臺北市重慶南路一段 61 號 (重南門市)
電　　話	(02)25006600
網　　址	三民網路書店 https://www.sanmin.com.tw
出版日期	初版一刷 2020 年 7 月
	初版二刷 2022 年 9 月
書籍編號	S806470
I S B N	978-957-14-6835-8

三民書局

READING POWER

Reading Power 系列

Intermediate

英文閱讀 High Five

翻譯與解析

王隆興 編著

主題 High 五大主題分類，學習有組織
文章 High 各大議題融入，閱讀有脈絡
題型 High 全新題型編寫，應試有實力
解析 High 逐題精闢講解，理解有效率
成績 High 全書完整複習，迎戰新題型

三民書局

Unit 1

寵物假期

　　假期來臨時，寵物飼主通常會面臨困難的抉擇。他們那毛茸茸的朋友可能無法跟著一起到海灘或自然保護區。狗與貓可能會將疾病傳染給野生動植物，而且牠們往往不喜歡長途車程。

　　德國動物保護聯盟提供了另一種替代方案。打著「你幫我照顧寵物，我也會幫你」的口號，提供服務讓飼主可以享受無憂無慮的假期。該項服務是將計畫出遊的寵物飼主與樂意收留出遊者寵物的人配對。飼主與「寵物保姆」會見面討論寵物的需求，並且飼主會支付保姆寵物飼料及照顧的費用，價格由保姆訂定，通常很低廉。飼主不在時，大部分的寵物都挺喜歡另一個家庭的陪伴。當保姆想要度假時，他們也可以利用該服務尋找照顧寵物的人。

　　寵物保姆也變得愈來愈流行。許多寵物飼主經常組織非正式的社群來照顧彼此的寵物。美國有一個社區就利用社群媒體來通知居民誰有空當寵物保姆。在許多其他社區裡，訊息則是靠口耳相傳。養了 2 隻狗的克莉絲塔‧史蒂芬 (Krista Stephens) 每次出遊都會雇用寵物保姆，她說：「這些小男生（她對狗的稱呼）似乎很喜歡這種體驗。知道有人好好照顧牠們，我就能放心了。」

解析

1. 本篇文章主要是介紹 **(D)** 當寵物的飼主外出旅行時，他們可以從哪些管道找到適合的保姆來看顧他們的毛小孩。

2. 本句提到狗和貓可能會傳染疾病給野生動物，而且牠們也不喜歡長途車程，因此可以得知 furry friends 所指的是 **(B)** 狗與貓。

3. 由第二段 ❸ 可以得知德國動物保護聯盟所提供的服務是協助配對有計畫出門遠行的寵物飼主以及願意接納照顧他人寵物的保姆。

4. 由第一段第二句可得知在自然保護區的入口處可能可以見到 **(C)**「寵物不得入內」的標誌。

5. 由第二段第二句聯盟的口號為「你照顧我的寵物，我也會幫你」以及同段的第七句可推知 **(C)** 當寵物保姆外出遠行時，他們也可以利用聯盟所提供的服務來幫自己的毛小孩找到保姆。

face　v.　面臨	tough　adj.　棘手的	roll around　（季節、假日等）到來
come along　跟隨	league　n.　聯盟	come up with　想出
alternative　n.　替代方案	carefree　adj.　無憂無慮的	match　v.　配對
sitter　n.　保姆	companionship　n.　陪伴	informal　adj.　非正式的
resident　n.　居民	available　adj.　有空的	by word of mouth　口耳相傳

1

Unit 2

鮭魚跳躍，棕熊饗宴

　　紅鮭的生命週期是一個完整的循環，在過程中牠們與捕食魚類的棕熊們會有一段驚奇的相遇。紅鮭出生在阿拉斯加，當牠們 2 歲之後，會在太平洋海域中漫遊 2 年，直到牠們的本能帶領牠們洄游。初夏時，上百萬隻成年的紅鮭會聚集在一起，湧進納克內克河 (Naknek River) 的淡水水域裡，然後到廣闊的納克內克湖 (Naknek Lake) 再度分散開來。過了這座湖，就很接近牠們的出生地——布魯克斯湖 (Brooks Lake) 了。然而，要回到牠們的出生地需要展現極大的精力及勇氣，牠們必須游過布魯克斯河 (Brooks River)，並得逆流躍上一座 6 呎高的瀑布，同時還得躲避來這裡捕魚嚐鮮的眾多巨大棕熊。

　　在布魯克斯瀑布 (Brooks Falls) 有一個觀景臺，讓遊客能目睹棕熊們等待捕食鮭魚的奇景。參觀時，遊客有機會看見多達 15 隻棕熊等在布魯克斯瀑布下，耐心的等著鮭魚躍上瀑布，落入牠們的嘴裡。鮭魚經常無法掌握適當角度，不但無法越過瀑布，反而掉進往下的水流中，只好重新來過。如果鮭魚在跳躍時太過接近棕熊，棕熊就會在半空中將牠抓住吞下去，藉此儲存脂肪來抵禦阿拉斯加漫長的冬天。如果棕熊發現水中有鮭魚，牠就會一頭跳進河裡，用巨大的熊掌把鮭魚抓到岩石附近，然後滿足的回到岸上，準備享用生魚片當作午餐。

　　儘管在旅途中會遇到這些危險，卻不能阻止紅鮭一再嘗試大跳躍，好回到牠們出生的寧靜水域裡，如此牠們才能在那裡孕育下一代，使生命生生不息。

解析

1. 由第一段第一句與最末句可以判斷出 (C) 棕熊是阿拉斯加紅鮭洄游返鄉時的最大威脅。
2. 第二段第四句 (B) 棕熊獵捕紅鮭是為了儲備足夠的脂肪來度過漫長的寒冬。
3. 由第二段的內文可得知棕熊會成群結隊地在瀑布下等候，為了享受自動送上門的紅鮭大餐，所以本題的錯誤敘述應為 (D) 如果棕熊看到了紅鮭，牠會眼睜睜地讓牠溜走。
4. 由第一段 ❷ 的敘述可以得知驅使紅鮭洄游到牠們的故鄉來產卵的原因是牠們的生物本能。
5. 由第一段內文可以得知阿拉斯加紅鮭的生命歷程為 (B) 鮭魚卵於阿拉斯加的布魯克斯湖中孵化，2 歲大的小魚會順游到太平洋並且在那裡成長茁壯直至繁殖年齡，初夏時牠們會大規模地集結逆流而上到達納克內克河，接著努力穿越納克內克湖，如此歷經千辛萬苦只為回到牠們的故鄉——布魯克斯湖。

encounter n. 相遇	instinct n. 本能	squeeze v. 擠入
enormous adj. 龐大的	bravery n. 勇敢	massive adj. 大量的
spectacle n. 景觀	await v. 等待	instead of 作為…的替代
dive v. 下潛	lcap v. 跳	grab v. 搶奪
paw n. 爪子	midst n. 當中	attempt v. 試圖

地鼠陸龜

　　陸地上的烏龜正確的名稱為陸龜 (tortoise)，牠們以陸地為家。全世界共有約 40 種不同品種的陸龜，包括了棲息在美國東南部自佛羅里達州到德州間沙地及林區裡的地鼠陸龜。

　　地鼠陸龜的特徵是擁有 8 到 15 吋的棕色龜殼和為了適合挖掘而變平的前肢。牠們以龜殼作為保護措施。陸龜可以將頭完全縮進殼裡，並用四肢將開口覆蓋住，這樣就沒有任何掠食者或人類可以傷害牠們。地鼠陸龜的一生以如隧道般的地洞為中心，這些地洞是牠們用像鏟子般的前肢挖掘而成的。那也是為何這些令人著迷的動物被稱為「地鼠」，牠們一生之中至少有 95% 的時間都在這些地洞裡度過。當冬天牠們在這些地洞中冬眠時，也可以保護自己不過度受寒。

　　地鼠陸龜以低矮植物為食，也吃莓果和其他季節性的水果。有幾種地鼠陸龜，像是德州地鼠陸龜，則會選擇一些較不可口的植物作為牠們的食物，如刺梨仙人掌。如同大部分陸上的烏龜，地鼠陸龜不會在池塘裡棲息，牠們天生就住在陸地上，而且不會游泳。牠們只需要一點點水來飲用及洗澡。即使 1 年多不碰水，成龜仍可存活下來。牠們所吸收的水大部分來自春季時攝取的植物中所含的水分。

　　陸龜通常很長壽，已知有些陸龜活了超過 100 年。因為陸龜能活得很久、具有古老的物種起源而且動作緩慢悠閒，所以牠們已成為智慧、堅毅和長壽的象徵。近來這些無害的動物數量已經減少了。土地發展已經對陸龜存活造成最嚴重的威脅。現今牠們受到（美國）聯邦保護，列為瀕臨絕種的物種。

解　析

1. 由第一段最後一行可以得知這種地鼠陸龜最常見於 **(D)** 美國東南方由佛羅里達州一直延伸到德州地區。
2. 由第二段 ❺ 可得知地鼠陸龜因為一生中有 95% 的時間都生活在地洞裡而得其名。
3. 本篇文章主要介紹地鼠陸龜的分布地區、生活習性、外貌特徵、種類分支以及象徵意義，因此最有可能出現在 **(D)** 介紹野生動物的電視節目上。
4. 本文於第四段倒數第二行指出 **(B)** 土地開發對於地鼠陸龜的生存造成最大的威脅。
5. 由第三段第五句可以得知地鼠陸龜是陸龜的一種，牠們不需要傍水而居也不會游泳，故 **(A)** 地鼠陸龜是游泳好手的敘述是錯誤的。

tortoise n. 陸龜	residence n. 居住	inhabit v. 棲息
flattened adj. 被弄平的	limb n. 肢（手或腳）	predator n. 掠食者
revolve around 以…為中心	dormant adj. 冬眠的	appetizing adj. 刺激食慾的
cacti n. （cactus 的複數形）仙人掌	intake n. 攝取	moisture n. 水分
persistence n. 堅毅	longevity n. 長壽	pose a threat to 對…造成威脅

動物如何溝通

　　動物有其天生、獨到的溝通方式。牠們的方式可能對我們而言很奇怪、很陌生，但卻很有效率及效果。例如，蜜蜂是以舞蹈溝通。偵察蜂每次搜尋結束回巢後，就會以 8 字型飛舞，告訴其他蜜蜂最新的食物來源在哪裡、如何到達、要飛行多久及食物的種類與品質。

　　牛羚也是以舞蹈溝通，但牠跳舞是表示牠今天不想被吃掉。當牛羚被掠食者追逐時，牠會先快跑一小段距離，然後轉身面向敵人。牠會來回擺頭與持續踏步。掠食者會被這種怪異的舞蹈所迷住並感到不解。不久牠就會放棄捕食了。畢竟，誰想吃一隻發瘋的牛羚呢？

　　打哈欠也是動物的溝通方式，但並不表示「我累了」。例如猴子打哈欠是要嚇唬敵人，牠們會對掠食者或敵對的猴子張嘴露牙。對猴子來說，打哈欠就表示 「我會咬人！」。河馬也會打哈欠，但卻是用來告訴別人誰是老大。河馬可以張開牠滿是巨牙的大嘴巴達 150 度之大！

　　動物有許多其他有效的溝通方式，包括姿勢、聲音、明亮的色彩、閃光與複雜的氣味。如果你花點時間研究動物的溝通，一定會很訝異我們周遭的世界有多複雜。

解　析

1. 本篇文章主要介紹動物與昆蟲所獨有的溝通方式，例如：蜜蜂和牛羚會跳舞、猴子與河馬會張大嘴巴打呵欠等，而最後一段也提到牠們也會利用姿勢、聲音、閃光、明亮的顏色或是氣味來表達，故 (D) 進食是唯一沒有提及的方式。

2. 第二段前一句提到牛羚會使用來回擺頭與持續踏步等特有的動作來迷亂 (B) 牠的捕食者，進而使捕食者失去對這個獵物的興趣。

3. 第一段的 ❹ 提到偵察蜂會利用「8 字舞」向同伴傳達最近的花蜜位置、如何到達、路途需要多少時間以及花蜜的品質與種類等資訊。

4. 本文作者是利用 (A) 提出許多動物與昆蟲的例子來佐證其主張：動物與昆蟲有許多獨一無二且有效的溝通方式，而這些方式在人類看來可能是怪異又陌生的。

5. 河馬張大嘴巴打呵欠是為了顯示自己的地位較高；蜜蜂以 8 字型態飛舞傳達與花蜜有關的資訊，而非跳 8 次舞，故只有 (C) 猴子打呵欠的動作是為了恫嚇對方的敘述是正確的。

communicate	v. 溝通	scout bee	偵察蜂	pattern	n. 圖案
wildebeest	n. 牛羚	pursue	v. 追捕	toss	v. 甩動
captivate	v. 使著迷	confuse	v. 使困惑	abandon	v. 放棄
for instance	例如	rival	adj. 敵對的	gesture	n. 姿勢
complex	adj. 複雜的	scent	n. 氣味	complexity	n. 複雜性

對抗世界飢餓的良方？

　　根據聯合國的報告，基因改造農作物可以解決部分的世界饑荒問題，然而，對於基因改造農作物是好是壞同時也有不少爭論。基因工程的擁護者說，基因改造的農作物比較容易栽種，更營養、好吃又耐久。添加維他命與蛋白質的蔬菜可以增加營養價值，而且聯合國糧農組織表示，抗旱及抗蟲害的農作物有助於供給日益成長的世界人口，並提升第三世界國家的所得。印度、菲律賓、中國、泰國及許多其他國家都已經種植了上百萬英畝的基因改造農作物了。

　　另一方面，基因改造食物的反對者則認為，雖然種植這類作物可以幫助對抗世界饑荒，但這並不是真正解決這項全球問題的周全之道，也許反而會帶給第三世界國家更多的問題。基因改造農作物不僅最終可能會對人體造成傷害，而且還可能經由花粉交換改變原生植物的多樣性。它們可能會以我們現今所無法預期的方式傷害環境，因為基因改造農作物的影響至今尚未完全研究透徹。

　　在歐洲，消費者反對基因改造食物上桌的聲浪相當強烈，以至於有些公司必須中止銷售基因改造農作物。然而，許多開發中國家仍對生物技術的神奇效果深信不疑，即使他們可能沒有適當的政策控制基因改造作物。世界饑荒與財富的分配比較有關，而與糧食生產不足比較無關。換句話說，窮人真正需要的是更容易取得土地、市場、教育及信貸系統的途徑，而非尚未證實對環境影響是好是壞的生物技術。

解析

1. 由作者於本文最後一段提到基改農作物這種生物技術對於環境的影響是好是壞都還是未知數來看，作者應該是對於基改食物抱持著 (D) 懷疑的態度。
2. 本篇文章的鋪陳先於第一段闡述了基改農作物的優點，而後於第二段講明其缺點，是採取 (D) 正反比較的架構。
3. 本句上文提到基改食物可能會為第三世界國家帶來更多的問題，因此可以推測本句會接著說明 (C) 基改食物可能會造成哪些問題。
4. 由第一段 ❹ 可得知添加維他命與蛋白質的蔬菜的好處是可以增加營養價值。
5. 由第二段第三句可得知基改食物會透過植物授粉的過程改變了原生植物的多樣性，故 (A) 的敘述有誤。

remedy n. 解決方法	genetically modified crop 基因改造農作物	genetic engineering 基因工程
nutrition n. 營養	drought n. 旱災	insect-resistant adj. 抗蟲害的
boost v. 增加	agriculture n. 農業	comprehensive adj. 全面的
consumer n. 消費者	opposition n. 反對	biotechnology n. 生物技術
starvation n. 飢餓	distribution n. 分配	inadequate adj. 不足的

吃人傳說

　　大部分的人認為鯊魚是危險的生物，等著吃落單的游泳者。事實上，75% 的鯊魚咬傷並不會造成傷者死亡，而且已知的 350 種鯊魚中，只有 32 種曾經攻擊人類！世界各地的研究已經有更多這樣的發現。

　　像是加拿大的 ReefQuest 鯊魚研究中心等機構的科學家已經推翻食人鯊的迷思。他們發現，最危險的鯊魚品種之一的大白鯊通常會把人吐出來，而不是吃進去。有些科學家認為，這是因為牠們不喜歡氯丁橡膠的味道，也就是大部分游泳者穿的潛水衣所用的橡膠材質。有人則認為鯊魚嫌人類骨瘦如柴，偏好肉質豐腴的海豹與海獅。

　　大部分的鯊魚並非因為喜食人肉而攻擊，牠們的攻擊通常是因為人類侵犯到牠們的領域或干擾牠們交配所引起的。而且游泳者在水中看起來很像海豹與海獅，若有戴珠寶首飾，在陽光下閃爍看起來就如同魚鱗一般，鯊魚可能因此把人誤認成海洋哺乳類動物而加以攻擊。另一種可能性則是鯊魚只是用嘴巴來增進對物體的了解，咬東西是基於好奇，並不是想致人於死地。

　　雖然鯊魚不會為覓食而攻擊人類，但牠們攻擊時都極為殘暴。例如白鯊會從游泳者背後暗伏而上，突然猛力一咬，造成嚴重傷害。所以遠離經常發生鯊魚咬傷事件的地方才是最安全的，例如海渠、河口及岸邊沙洲後方的淺水海域。尊重鯊魚的領域及兇殘的威力才是確保你安全上岸的最佳方法。

解　析

1. 本篇文章的目的在於 (A) 釐清一些跟鯊魚喜歡吃人有關的迷思，除了提到鯊魚其實不愛吃人肉的原因之外，也列出幾項會驅使鯊魚主動攻擊人類的合理推測。
2. 由第四段的敘述可得知避開鯊魚攻擊最安全的方式是 (D) 遠離牠們棲息的領域，因為鯊魚的攻擊通常是出於人類侵犯其領域。
3. 由第三段最末句可得知鯊魚咬人是出於好奇心而非意在致人於死，故 (C) 的敘述是錯誤的。
4. 第四段 ❸ 指出鯊魚的攻擊好發於海渠、河口與岸邊沙洲後方的淺水海域。
5. 本句提到鯊魚的攻擊通常是由人類侵犯其領域或是干擾牠們的交配活動所引發的，故本題答案為 (C) 造成。

conduct v. 實施	facility n. 設施	myth n. 迷思
neoprene n. 氯丁二烯橡膠	bony adj. 骨瘦如柴的	flesh n. 肉
prompt v. 引起	territory n. 領域	resemble v. 與…相像
glint v. 閃閃發亮	mammal n. 哺乳動物	out of curiosity 出於好奇
inflict v. 給予（傷害等）	sandbar n. 沙洲	ferocious adj. 凶猛的

訓練小狗居家方便習慣

　　抱起來柔軟、有雙大眼、可愛的腳掌、生性好玩的小狗令人喜愛。牠們人見人愛，每年有上百萬人帶小狗回家，如果你已經是其中一員，你一定了解教導寵物在適當地點方便的過程能把你對狗兒的情感迅速變成挫折感。這裡有幾個教你如何訓練你的寵物的建議，有助於雙方維持和睦的關係。

　　首先，在戶外選擇某處作為小狗的廁所。如果所選的區域地表比較特別，像是草地、碎石子地、水泥地或沙地，牠會更容易學習。然後，要經常讓牠有機會到那兒去。你可以在那個區域圍個圍欄，天氣好時可以讓牠待在那裡，或是每天無論晴雨都帶牠到那個特別的區域待上至少 45 分鐘。只要牠在正確的地方方便，就可以摸摸牠、低聲逗牠，大大稱讚一番，說牠有多聰明、多棒。

　　夜間或你不在家時，則把小狗圍在家中的小區域內，在裡頭鋪上紙，可以的話也放上觸感類似牠的廁所表面的東西：草屑、砂礫或細沙，當牠想方便時，就會到那兒去方便。小心千萬不要讓寵物在地板或地毯上方便。當牠想這麼做時，趕快抱牠到鋪紙的特定地方。時間久了，牠就會養成只在正確地方方便的習慣。不過要記得，不管你教得多努力，至少要花 6 個月，你的小狗才能學會正確遵守此居家習慣。

解析

1. 本篇文章的主旨在於 **(B)** 介紹訓練狗狗定點方便的一些要領與訣竅。
2. (A)(B)(D) 選項都是方便的意思，只有 **(C)** 柔情地低語與另外三者不同。
3. 第三段 **7** 指出狗狗至少需要 6 個月才能完全學會定點方便的行為。
4. 由第二段第二句及第三段第四句可以看出，草地、沙地或是碎石子地都是訓練狗狗如廁的適合地點，唯有 **(D)** 室內地毯是絕對不行的。
5. 由第二段第四句可得知不論晴天或是雨天，飼主每天應該起碼花費 45 分鐘帶狗狗到戶外設定好的據點讓牠們活動與方便，故 **(A)** 的敘述有誤。

housebreak　v.　訓練寵物居家方便習慣	cuddly　adj.　令人想摟抱的	frustration　n.　挫折
eliminate　v.　排除（廢物）	distinctive　adj.　特殊的	concrete　n.　水泥
constant　adj.　持續的	pen　n.　（家禽、家畜等的）圍欄	coo　v.　輕聲說
excrete　v.　方便	confine　v.　限制	grass clippings　草屑
urge　n.　衝動	alert　adj.　警覺的	relieve　v.　排尿

Unit 8
人類最凶猛的對手如何變成最好的朋友

　　在當今世界，狗在人們的生活中扮演著重要的角色。牠們與人類並肩生活，在我們生活的各個方面都陪伴著，包括狩獵、趕牲口、交通以及單純成為寵物。然而，狗並不是自古就與人類那麼親近。從歷史上看，狗源自灰狼，牠們過去經常與人類爭奪食物。狼生活在大群體中，牠們的家庭結構與人類相似。

　　人類對狼曾經是巨大的威脅，儘管脫離狼群而居的狼學習到，如果牠們不主動侵略，牠們就可與人類更親近並吃人類的食物。這些較溫馴的狼活得更長久，並且這個基因得以傳承下來。牠們被人類用來找其他人或事物的蹤跡並防範危險。慢慢地，狼開始了解人類的命令。在 32,000 年前，第一隻狗出現了。牠們看起來像狼，但身體、鼻子和牙齒比較小。隨著人類生活的改變，狗也適應了新環境與新工作。矮胖的狗被用來放牧動物；長而瘦的狗幫助將狐狸趕出洞；瘦狗被用來賽跑；最後，肌肉發達的狗被用來看管門戶。

　　現今我們所認識的狗最初出現在維多利亞時代的英格蘭。狗因為外型而被人工養殖，並且被分為不同的品種。今日，由於這種人工繁殖，其中一些狗罹患了健康問題，例如背部問題和呼吸困難。狗在短時間內經歷了巨大的變化。人類的生活已經經歷許多變革，狗同樣也是。狗與人類之間有著相互的愛與尊重。因此，在未來的幾年中，狗可能依然會是人類最好的朋友。

解析

1. 根據第二段的敘述，不同身型的狗可以擔任不同類型的工作，體型偏瘦者適合參加賽跑；矮胖結實者可以勝任趕牲口的工作；肌肉發達者可以看管門戶而瘦長型者可以把狐狸趕出洞穴。

shape	job
slim	racing
short, stocky	herding animals
muscular	guardians
long, thin	chase foxes out of holes

2. 由本文最後兩句提到「人類與狗彼此相互關愛尊重，因此狗將來仍然會是人類最好的朋友」來看，最適合描述兩者之間關係者應該是 (C) 合作。

3. 第二段先提及人類與狗的祖先──狼之間本是競爭的關係，其中性情比較溫順的狼的基因綿延下去，在 32,000 年前誕生了第一隻狗，而狗與人一樣也在不斷地改變，由此可知本段是以 (D) 時間發生先後順序的方式來敘述。

4. 由第二段第五句之後的敘述可以看到，第一隻狗出現於 32,000 年前；現代狗的體型比牠們的祖先──狼要來得小一點、牙齒也沒那麼尖；現代狗因為身型不同而有不同的任務與工作，故本題只有 (B) 的敘述無誤。

5. 第一段 ❷ 提到狗在許多方面陪伴人類的日常生活，像打獵、趕牲口、交通或單純當寵物而已。

fierce	adj. 猛烈的	rival	n. 敵手	accompany	v. 陪伴
herd	v. 放牧	transportation	n. 運輸	threat	n. 威脅
tame	adj. 溫順的	gene	n. 基因	command	n. 指令
adapt	v. 適應	stocky	adj. 矮壯的，結實的	breed	v. （為育種目的）飼養
suffer	v. 受折磨	massive	adj. 巨大的	mutual	adj. 相互的

Unit 9

翅膀——當鳥只能振翅不能飛

　　有超過 40 種不會飛的鳥生活在地球上，包括澳洲內陸、非洲熱帶莽原和南極大陸。牠們的種類包括企鵝、鴕鳥、鷸鴕和鴯鶓。儘管如此，這些鳥還是找到了其他的生存方式，例如使用鋒利的爪子攻擊競爭對手。

　　能夠飛翔是鳥類的優勢。牠們能夠逃離危險、能夠狩獵並且可以移動到遠處。然而飛行也會引發問題。舉例來說，飛行消耗大量能量。此外，它限制了鳥的體型和體重。如果鳥不飛，牠就能以營養少的食物為生，例如來自紐西蘭的短翅水雞就是吃山上的草。

　　如果鳥類沒有飛行的壓力，牠們可以在幾世代後停止飛行。例如，如果牠們飛往一個沒有地面威脅的島嶼，牠們可能就不再飛行。牠們的身體在數百萬年中緩慢變化。牠們的骨頭變得越來越粗，牠們的背部肌肉萎縮甚至消失。當人類到達並帶來其他動物時，會對這些不會飛的鳥造成問題。在紐西蘭，歐洲人帶來了白鼬，這導致許多本土鳥類瀕臨絕種。

　　像鴯鶓和鴕鳥這種不會飛的大型鳥已經數百萬年沒有飛過，但由於牠們的大小而得以倖存；體重和肌肉，會幫助牠們奔跑。所以如果鳥不能飛，牠們會用翅膀來做什麼？這些鳥已經調整翅膀適應成其他用途。企鵝用翅膀游泳，而鴯鶓用翅膀保護著蛋。所以即使這些鳥不會飛，牠們仍然可以成功存活。

解析

1. 第二段 ❷ 提到鳥類能夠飛翔的優點像是避開危險、獵捕食物及移動到遠處等。
2. 第三段最末句提到歐洲人將白鼬帶入紐西蘭，造成當地許多不會飛的原生鳥類瀕臨滅亡，由此可以推論出 (A) 人類的活動對於一些無法飛行的鳥類造成巨大的威脅。
3. 本篇文章主要探討引發鳥類失去飛翔本能的原因、變成不會飛翔的鳥類會有哪些變化與牠們的生存之道，因此最有可能出現在 (B) 與動物有關的紀錄片之中。
4. 「紐西蘭的短翅水雞可以吃山上的雜草過活」，作者使用這個例子來佐證 (D) 當鳥類失去飛翔的能力後，牠們就不需要依靠營養價值高的食物生存。
5. 第一段有提到，企鵝、鷸鴕與都是無法飛行的鳥類。而 (C) 白鼬並不是鳥類，而是造成鳥類瀕臨絕種的動物。

flap v. （振）翅	Antarctic n. 南極地區	ostrich n. 鴕鳥
kiwi n. 鷸鴕，奇異鳥	emu n. 鴯鶓	claw n. （獸或鳥類的）爪
competitor n. 競爭者	consume v. （尤指大量地）消耗	nourishment n. 營養
feather n. 羽毛	fluff n. 絨毛	shrink v. （使）變小
stoat n. 白鼬	endangered adj. 瀕危的	shelter v. 保護；躲避

9

動物能互相欺騙嗎？

　　據說動物和人是相似的，但是就像人類可以狡猾並互相說謊以得到他們想要的東西一樣，動物也會這樣做嗎？公螢火蟲會發光以吸引母的，而另一品種的母螢火蟲會向公的閃回，以誘使牠靠近以吃掉牠。科學家一直在研究動物是否會試圖欺騙另一個動物。有 3 個步驟可以確認，首先，動物必須成功愚弄另一隻動物。然後，該動物必須從中獲得一些好處。最後，這個行為絕不可以是偶然的。

　　動物使用不同的方式互相欺騙。葉尾壁虎和章魚等某些動物會融入周圍，因此其他動物看不到牠們。這稱為偽裝。其他像猩紅王蛇這樣的動物經過了幾代的演化適應，形成了與具有劇毒的金黃珊瑚蛇相似的條紋。這使其他動物搞混了兩種蛇，以為牠們都有劇毒並因而遠離。這被稱為模仿。還有另一種動物試圖互相欺騙的方法是改變其行為模式。例如，當變色龍知道附近有鳥時，牠們會改變體色消失在背景環境中。

　　叉尾卷尾鳥是另一種使用獨特方法欺騙他人的動物。牠們發出一種警報聲，警告其他動物鄰近的危險。有時牠們會發出假的警報，而使用它的真正原因是從其他動物那裡偷食物。如果你觀察牠們的行為和結果，則可以快速了解牠們的真正動機。

解析

1. 第二段第一、二句提到這種將自己完全融入周遭環境以躲避敵人攻擊的方式就叫做「偽裝」，故選 (B) Camouflaging（偽裝）。
2. 根據文章敘述，第三段提到叉尾卷尾鳥發出假警報聲以偷得其他動物的食物；第二段最後提到變色龍改變體色來躲避鳥類；第一段提到母螢火蟲發出閃光是為了捕食，只有 (D) 進攻其他動物的棲息地並未出現在文章中。
3. 第二段提到 (C) 猩紅王蛇演化出與含有劇毒的金黃珊瑚蛇相似的花紋來保護自己。
4. 第一段的最後以 (A) 學者專家的定義作為結束，認為動物或是昆蟲若使用欺敵之術，那必定是有意愚弄對方而非偶然，而且還可從中獲取利益。
5. 由第二段可得知變色龍的獨門欺敵之術乃是「改變體色使自己消失於背景環境中」；由第三段可得知叉尾卷尾鳥使用欺敵之術是為了「偷得其他動物的食物」。

	unique ways of tricking others	purposes
Chameleons	changing color to vanish into the background	to avoid birds
Fork-tailed drongos	raising a false alarm	to steal food from other animals

trick v. 欺騙	cunning adj. 狡猾的	attract v. 吸引
species n. 物種	gecko n. 壁虎	blend into 混入
surroundings n. 環境	camouflage v. 偽裝	stripe n. 條紋
Eastern Coral snake 金黃珊瑚蛇	poisonous adj. 有毒的，有害的	mimicry n. 模仿
chameleon n. 變色龍	approach v. 臨近；靠近	motivation n. 動機

向母親致敬

　　母親在全世界人民的心中佔有特殊的地位，許多地方都有特殊的日子來對她們表示敬意。

　　最早關於母親的慶祝活動是古希臘節慶儀式的一部分，以迎接春天的到來並向眾神之母瑞亞 (Rhea) 致敬。後來，在 17 世紀時，英國人發展出一種習俗來慶祝「拜望雙親日」。人們通常會放假，以便他們可以探訪他們的「母教堂」，也就是該地區的主要教堂。每年的這一天回到母教堂，並與自己的母親和其他家庭成員團聚被認為是相當重要的一件事。最終，「拜望雙親日」成為整個歐洲和英屬群島的人們對母教堂與母親表達敬意的日子。

　　在美國，一位名叫安娜‧賈維斯 (Ana Jarvis) 的女子，提議應該設立一個特別的節日，以用來致敬全國的母親。她寫信給全國各地的教堂和商業領袖，鼓勵他們在自己的社區慶祝母親節。在 1908 年的 5 月 10 日這天，她的家鄉西維吉尼亞州 (West Virginia) 慶祝了第一個母親節。這個節日因此開始變得普遍，而在 1914 年時，每年 5 月的第二個星期天被命名為美國官方的母親節。

　　許多其他國家也慶祝母親節，包括瑞典、墨西哥、澳洲、日本、中國、加拿大及新加坡等。小孩和大人與母親一起慶祝這特別的日子，並送上鮮花和糖果作為禮物來感謝母親的愛與仁慈。

解析

1. 本篇文章的主旨在於 **(C)** 敘述母親節的歷史起源，並且提到美國將 5 月的第二個星期天訂定為母親節的由來。

2. 由於 5 月的第二個星期天為母親節，在圖中即為 5 月 13 日，本題中的珍 (Jane) 與傑 (Jay) 想要在母親節的前一天為媽媽與祖母慶祝母親節，所以勾選答案 **May 12**（5 月 12 日）。

3. 由第二段看來，英國人可以在「拜望雙親日」放假一天，並且在當天去參拜家鄉最主要的教堂與探望自己的雙親，而這個節日後來也傳遍歐洲與英國各地，故本題只有 **(D)** 由美國最早開始慶祝這個節日的敘述是錯誤的。

4. 第二段 ❶ 中有提到瑞亞乃是眾神之母。

5. 根據第三段第三句，安娜‧賈維斯的故鄉——西維吉尼亞州是美國第一個於 1908 年開始慶祝母親節的地方，而非將 5 月的第二個星期天訂定為母親節，故本題 **(C)** 的敘述有誤。

honor v. 向…致敬	festival n. 節慶	custom n. 習俗
celebrate v. 慶祝	reunite v. 使重聚	eventually adv. 最終
throughout prep. 遍及	propose v. 提議	set aside 撥出
encourage v. 鼓勵	community n. 社區	hometown n. 家鄉
widespread adj. 普遍的	official adj. 官方的	kindness n. 仁慈

Unit 12

駱駝圖書館

你會願意跟駱駝借書嗎?在肯亞,國家圖書館服務局組織了一個流動圖書館,前往偏遠的村莊。他們使用了駱駝來跋涉到車輛無法行駛的地方。但是駱駝圖書館的想法從何而來呢?

肯亞政府於 1965 年成立了肯亞國家圖書館服務局 (knls)。由於肯亞大部分的人口居住在偏遠的村莊而非城市,因此流動圖書館的必要性很快就被重視。該組織在自行車、摩托車、汽車或卡車上堆放一箱一箱的書,組建了許多流動圖書館。目的是希望提升該國的識字率。

然而,肯亞的東北省從來都不是一個非常安全的地方。高速公路上的搶劫非常普遍,連摩托車騎士都被建議在旅行時結伴成行。學校的書籍是如此的珍貴,強盜甚至會搶劫小學。警察必須駐紮在每個城鎮的入口,以保護城鎮免遭這些小偷的襲擊。像加里薩 (Garissa) 這樣的地方,不但有強盜,地形又險峻,連最耐操的車輛都無法抵達。

所以在 1996 年,加里薩的圖書館員偉克力夫‧歐羅克 (Wycliffe Oluoch) 便組建了第一個駱駝圖書館,由三隻駱駝組成,一隻馱著很多書,一隻馱著帳篷和圖書館員的辦公桌,而另一隻則備用於緊急情況。駱駝很容易適應惡劣的天氣和崎嶇的地形,在幾乎沒有喝水的情況下也可以走很長的距離。每個社區都必須取得資格才能得到駱駝圖書館的拜訪,合格的社區必須是永久性而非臨時性的居住地。社區內必須有一所學校並有一個正職的校長,並且有對這些書本負有責任的老師們。如果社區丟失了一本書,他們將失去使用駱駝圖書館的權利。

對於肯亞的許多孩子來說,駱駝圖書館為他們帶來了他們在課堂外閱讀的第一本書。一些孩子喜歡經典小說。其他人喜歡關於科學和算術的書。駱駝圖書館逐步幫助了知識在全國的傳播,為以前難以抵達的地方,帶來了新希望。

解析

1. 由第四段敘述可得知駱駝圖書館是 (C) 由 3 隻駱駝馱著書長途跋涉到偏鄉提供圖書服務的流動圖書館。
2. 第三段第三句指出書是很珍貴的物品,連強盜也會襲擊學校來搶走書籍,由此可推論出 (B) 駱駝圖書館對於肯亞人而言是很珍貴的存在。
3. 由第三段第四句可得知警方在城鎮入口把守站崗的目的是 (A) 為了保護該鎮免於盜匪襲擊。
4. 第四段 ❶ 中提到偉克力夫‧歐羅克是一手催生了駱駝圖書館的人。
5. 由第四段第一句可得知駱駝流動圖書館由三隻駱駝組成,其中一隻負責馱著書本,另一隻負責馱著帳篷與圖書館員的辦公桌,而剩下的那一隻則是備用的駱駝,因此 (C) 的敘述有誤。

camel n. 駱駝	mobile adj. 流動式的	remote adj. 偏遠的
vehicle n. 車輛	majority n. 大多數	assemble v. 集合
heaping adj. 堆滿的	literacy n. 識字	bandit n. 強盜
emergency n. 緊急情況	harsh adj. 嚴酷的	qualify v. 有資格
permanent adj. 永久的	temporary adj. 臨時的	arithmetic n. 算術

從恰圖蘭卡到西洋棋

　　西洋棋已經在世界各地流傳了好幾個世紀了，但是它的起源卻因為歷史的重量而變得模糊。據了解在 6 世紀時印度人玩過類似的遊戲，名為恰圖蘭卡 (chaturanga)，這可能就是現代西洋棋的前身。這遊戲可能是經由印度和波斯之間的文化交流，或是當阿拉伯入侵波斯和部分歐洲地中海地區時而傳播到歐洲和世界其他地區。在接下來的千年裡，遊戲不斷演變，但依舊保留了我們今日所知的大致面貌。

　　國王、王后、主教、騎士和兵卒是西洋棋的棋子，並代表了中世紀歐洲的社會階級。棋盤可以被用作為中世紀歐洲社會的隱喻。每種棋子都有自己的移動方式，幾乎沒有例外。

　　西洋棋早期主要為貴族的遊戲，他們藉由贏棋所需要的數學分析，來訓練他們的軍事技巧和攻擊策略。如今，西洋棋已不再是專屬於貴族的遊戲了。它已經成為一種廣泛流行的消遣，同時也是普通大眾之間的激烈競賽。儘管大部分現代的棋手並不熟悉西洋棋的起源和歷史，但 21 世紀的棋手仍採用與中世紀貴族相同的策略。每個玩家的目標都是相同的：「將軍」。這是當對手的國王受到俘虜威脅而無處可逃時，己方便獲勝的情況。在現實生活中，這可能是一個帝國的終結。在遊戲中，敗方可以放棄遊戲，讓國王免受戰敗的屈辱。這可能是遊戲和現實生活間最大的差異之處。

解析

1. 根據第一段 ❷ 的敘述，6 世紀的印度遊戲——恰圖蘭卡很有可能就是現今西洋棋的起源。

2. 第三段第五句提到每個西洋棋的玩家都有一個共同的目標：「將軍」，意思是 (A) 把對手的國王逼到無處可逃，使其不得不認輸。

3. 第三段第二句與第三句提到西洋棋已不再是專屬貴族的遊戲了，現在的西洋棋是 (C) 廣受歡迎且一般人都可以盡情對戰的遊戲了。

4. 第一段第三句提到西洋棋的傳播與印度、波斯之間的文化交流或是與阿拉伯人入侵波斯與歐洲地中海地區息息相關，故只有 (A) 印度征服阿拉伯是錯誤的。

5. 第三段第四句提到大部分的現代棋手並不熟悉西洋棋的起源與歷史，故 (D) 的敘述有誤。

origin n. 起源	obscure v. 使模糊不清	interchange n. 交流
invasion n. 侵略	Mediterranean adj. 地中海的	evolve v. 演變
medieval adj. 中古世紀的	metaphor n. 暗喻	strategy n. 策略
reference n. 淵源	aristocrat n. 貴族	opponent n. 對手
empire n. 帝國	resign v. 放棄	humiliation n. 屈辱

飲茶文化

　　茶在華人的生活中一直扮演著重要的角色。人們對它的熱情激發了許多著名的藝術創作。李白、杜甫和白居易等傳奇詩人創作了許多關於茶的詩。著名畫家唐伯虎和文徵明甚至繪製了專門獻給這種飲料的畫作。

　　在西元 8 世紀之前，茶主要被當作藥物。茶葉中含有多種化學物質，這些化學物質被視為治療發炎和酸痛的有效方法。它還含有對消化和神經系統有幫助的刺激性物質。茶在魏晉南北朝時期逐漸發展成為一種常見的飲料。後來，在唐代，茶已內化為社會的固有象徵。不僅有專門的茶具，有關茶的書籍也陸續出版，其中包括最著名的陸羽的《茶經》。茶葉的種植和加工技術迅速發展，因此研發了許多著名的茶。如今有很多種茶，像是烏龍茶、普洱茶、龍井茶等。通過貿易，茶遍及了全球。

　　如今，茶不僅是一種飲料，還是華人文化中重要的一環。人們非常注重茶及其飲用方式。他們對茶葉的品質、烹茶時使用的水以及所搭配的茶具有嚴格的要求。在友好的對談、家庭聚會或重要的商務會議期間，喝茶是必不可缺的。簡而言之，茶已經成為數百年來備受推崇的寶藏。

解析

1. 根據第二段 ❶ 的敘述，茶原本被當作是一味藥材來使用。
2. 第一段第二句提到李白、白居易、杜甫都曾經創作過與茶有關的詩，而本題中的 (A) 唐伯虎應該是畫家。
3. 第二段第五句與第六句提到陸羽的《茶經》乃是於 (B) 唐朝時問世。
4. 第三段第三句提到人們對於茶葉的品質、烹茶時所使用的水以及品茶時所搭配的茶具都非常講究，故 (D) 水對於泡一杯好茶影響不大的敘述有誤。
5. 由第三段可得知茶對於華人而言已經不只是一種飲料，更是文化與日常生活的一部分，處處皆有它的存在，故本題答案為 (B)。

passion n. 熱情	inspire v. 激發	prominent adj. 卓越的
legendary adj. 著名的	dedicate to 獻給…	beverage n. 飲料
primarily adv. 主要地	inflammation n. 發炎	digestion n. 消化
inherent adj. 固有的	specialized adj. 專門的	advance v. 進步
requirement n. 要求	essential adj. 必要的	gathering n. 聚會

與環境和諧共處

　　「你的事業有困難或有戀愛的麻煩嗎？你問題的根源可能在於你房屋的設計。」中國古代哲學——風水的支持者說著。風水專家認為，一切都具有「氣」的能量，會影響環境和人類。根據風水的哲學，氣有 5 種：金、木、水、火和土。這些元素的不同組合將對我們與環境之間的關係產生重要的影響。風水哲學的最終目標是實現人與環境之間的和諧。

　　風水的主要作法是擺設周圍的事物，讓「氣」達到理想的狀態。它不僅涉及都市、村莊和建築物的規劃，還涉及室內設計。例如風水建議使用綠色的植物和漂亮的裝飾品來使你的空間變得愉悅，或保持房屋和工作場所的整潔。灰塵會損害你的健康並降低工作能力。另一個建議是選擇正確的家具擺設。例如，避免睡覺或坐著時背對著門。它起源於人們害怕野生動物或敵人闖入大門的時代。我們仍然具備這樣的本能，當我們休息時無法觀察到入口，會感到不舒服。

　　如今，風水不僅在華人中，同時在全世界的西方人中也得到了廣泛的實踐。比爾‧蓋茲 (Bill Gates) 和瑪丹娜 (Madonna) 等許多名人已經成為風水的粉絲。銀行和辦公樓，例如著名的川普大廈，都是按照這種古老的中國哲學的原理建造和裝飾。風水書籍銷往世界各地，風水顧問在許多西方城市設有辦公室。全世界的人們都開始使用風水以充分利用氣，並為他們的思想和環境帶來和平與和諧。

解析

1. 本篇文章的主旨在於介紹中國的古老哲學——風水，並且探討 (B) 利用風水的原理使人與環境能達到和諧共榮。
2. 根據第三段的敘述，不管是國內或國外，風水之道是一門顯學，與風水相關的書在世界各地都有銷售，由此可知 (C) 信奉風水者僅限於名人的說法有誤。
3. 第一段 ❹ 提到氣有五種：金、木、水、火、土。
4. 第二段第五句及第六句提到擺設家具的位置很重要，例如：人在睡覺或是坐著的時候應盡量不要背對門，根據圖片可以判斷出本題只有 (D) 選項的椅子背對著門。
5. 本文的第二段提到 (B) 許多風水應用在日常生活的例子，像是可以利用綠色的植栽來美化環境以及保持家裡與工作環境的整齊乾淨等。

harmony	n.	和諧	specialist	n.	專家	crucial	adj.	關鍵的
ultimate	adj.	最終的	desirable	adj.	渴望獲得的	interior	adj.	內部的
recommend	v.	建議	clutter	n.	雜亂	originate from		起源於
observe	v.	觀察	celebrity	n.	名人	principle	n.	原則
consultant	n.	顧問	make the best use of		善加利用	surroundings	n.	周遭環境

Unit 16

瞎扯——妨礙議事發言的由來

　　美國參議員一直以來常會進行所謂「妨礙議事發言」的冗長演講，來延誤或妨礙其他參議員進行法案表決。這種浪費時間的策略，是利用參議院允許議員對法案可進行無限時辯論的規定。只要參議員保持發言並繼續講話，新的議程就無法被討論，直到他或她講完為止。儘管參議院有制定其他規則來避免發表冗長的演說，但參議員可能會把他們說話的權利發揮到極致。

　　據說 "filibuster"（發表冗長的演說）這個字來自於荷蘭文——"vrijbuiter"，意為 16 世紀的「加勒比海盜」。在 19 世紀，"filibuster" 被用來形容革命軍與游擊隊員，到了 1850 年代，則有了現今的含意。目前 "filibuster" 被用來隱喻為政客用長篇演說來「劫持」議會。

　　一些政治家以發表長篇演說而聞名，一些妨礙議事的發言則因長度和毫無意義的內容而出名。在 1930 年代，休伊・朗 (Huey P. Long) 曾經霸佔議會長達 15 小時，朗誦美國憲法及他最愛的牡蠣與水餃食譜。最後因為他不得不離席去上廁所而失去發言權。迄今為止，參議員有史以來最長的演說是 1957 年參議員史壯・瑟蒙 (Strom Thurmond) 因反對民權法案而發表的演說。這位南方的參議員講了 24 小時 18 分鐘。真的是太會扯了！

解析

1. 第二段最末句提到「filibuster」這個字現在的意思是指美國的參議員以冗長乏味的演說來「劫持」議會，而第一段第一句提到他們這麼做是為了阻撓法案表決的進行，故本題答案為 (C)。

2. 由第二段第二句可知「filibuster」是從 (C) 1850 年代後才開始轉變為現在的意思。

3. 第一段第三句提到 (B) 只要美國參議員站上發言臺演說，他們就可以想說多久就說多久。

4. 根據第二段第一句的敘述，「filibuster」這個字在 16 世紀時所指的是「加勒比海的海盜」；同段第二句提到在 19 世紀時，這個字被借指為「革命軍與游擊隊員」，到了 1850 年代，「filibuster」變成是「政客以進行冗長演說的方式來劫持參議會發言臺」的暗喻。

	the meaning
sixteenth century	It was used for meaning pirates in the Caribbean.
nineteenth century	It was borrowed to describe revolutionaries and guerilla fighters.
1850s	It was a metaphor for politicians "hijacking" Senate debates with long speeches.

5. 第三段第一句提到有些相當出名的「filibuster」以其演說的長度與毫無重點的內容而流傳後世，由此可以推知本題答案為 (A) 沒有實質意義或事實的空談。

filibuster　n.　妨礙議事發言	senator　n.　參議員	long-winded　adj.　冗長的
colleague　n.　同事	extreme　n.　極限	pirate　n.　海盜
revolutionary　n.　革命人士	guerilla　n.　游擊隊	hijack　v.　劫持
legendary　adj.　傳奇的	content　n.　內容	constitution　n.　憲法
recipe　n.　食譜	excuse oneself　請求離去	on record　記錄上

Unit 17

寵物石風潮

　　1975 年的 4 月，美國廣告文案撰稿人蓋瑞・戴爾 (Gary Dahl) 與朋友們聊到養狗和貓等寵物有多麼不便。他開玩笑說，石頭會是最完美的寵物——個性安靜、乖巧，不需要食物、水或運動。有了這個簡單但原始的想法，戴爾發明了有史以來最奇怪的時尚之一——寵物石 (Pet Rock)，並在一夜之間成為百萬富翁。

　　寵物石基本上是一塊普通的圓形石頭，戴爾只花了一分錢來購買每一塊石頭。石頭被包裝在一個看起來像寵物提籃的盒子裡，附有一張幽默的使用說明手冊。該說明手冊由戴爾本人撰寫，內容包括有關如何訓練和照顧寵物石、寵物石的「品種」、服從訓練以及教它們進行攻擊。

　　8 月時，蓋瑞・戴爾開始在禮品展上販售他的「新發明」。富有創意的包裝和幽默的說明手冊吸引了很多人的注意。10 月時，他每天售出近一萬顆寵物石。到了 1975 年的聖誕節，他以每個 3.95 美元的價格賣出了超過 100 萬顆寵物石！不意外地，到了新的一年，大多數美國人已經厭倦了他們的「寵物石」（畢竟它們只是石頭而已），寵物石風潮像所有風潮一樣，一開始火速流行並急速退燒。

　　許多人將他視為天才。其他人看著寵物石的熱潮，難以置信地搖搖頭，不敢相信這麼多人願意將得來不易的錢花在一塊普通的石頭上。

解析

1. 根據第二段第四句的敘述，這本育石手冊上提到飼主應如何訓練和照顧石頭、寵物石的品種、馴服石頭的方法並且教導石頭進行攻擊，故只有 (C) 訓練石頭如廁這一項並沒有出現在手冊中。
2. 第一段最末句中提到蓋瑞・戴爾帶起將石頭當成寵物飼養的這股風潮，而第二段則是講述他如何將石頭加以包裝成擬真寵物，故可以推知第三段提到的「新發明」應該是指 (A) 寵物石。
3. 第一段最末句提到 (B) 蓋瑞・戴爾因為這個賣寵物石的創新點子而一夜致富，變成百萬富翁。
4. 第三段提到寵物石於 1975 年 8 月上市開賣，到了 1976 年新年期間飼養寵物石的熱潮就退了，「畢竟它們只是石頭而已」，由此可推知 (D) 作者並不意外寵物石的熱潮消失得這麼快。
5. 第一段第二句提到石頭「個性安靜、乖巧」又不需要「食物、水或運動」，是最完美的寵物。

the personality traits of a stone	What doesn't a stone need to survive?
quiet, well-behaved	food, water, or exercise

craze　n.　狂熱	inconvenient　adj.　帶來不便的	fad　n.　風潮
millionaire　n.　百萬富翁	overnight　adv.　一夜之間	average　adj.　普通的
package　v.　包裝	pet carrier　寵物提籃	breed　n.　品種
obedience　n.　服從	humorous　adj.　幽默的	instruction　n.　操作指南
hold sb. up as　推舉某人為…	disbelief　n.　不相信	hard-earned　adj.　辛苦賺來的

歐洲難民危機

　　敘利亞內戰已經導致大量難民越境逃往歐洲。隨著轟炸和戰爭在他們的家鄉繼續蔓延，成千上萬的敘利亞人發現他們最好的生存機會在自己的國家之外。不幸的是，並非所有歐洲聯盟（歐盟）成員國都張開雙臂歡迎難民。

　　敘利亞難民危機對歐盟成員國之間的政治發展有著嚴峻的影響。德國、丹麥和瑞典等國家有運行良好的系統可為難民尋找住所和工作，願意並有能力歡迎更多的難民。歐盟的一些成員，包括匈牙利、波蘭和波羅的海地區的小國家，由於財務能力較弱，較不願意接納難民。他們認為不應該被期望接納更多難民，因為他們擔心太多的移民會引起公民之間的衝突。當難民人數增長過快時，一些東歐國家會關閉國門，讓他們處於幾乎沒有食物和水的危急狀況之中。這些政治發展的風向導致的不幸，就是有數千位難民流離失所。

　　儘管敘利亞內戰證明無法遏制某些衝突，但人們仍將採取一切必要措施來讓家人安全。全世界需要儘早努力，以便於有需要的人能夠盡快找到庇護所。不只歐盟的成員需要共同努力，其他國家，像是美國需要採取行動並提供幫助。敘利亞難民值得全世界的憐憫。世界各國領袖應儘早放下彼此的不同論調，一起拯救生命。

解析

1. 第二段第二句與第三句中提到歐盟各國對於敘利亞難民的接納程度不同，富有的國家如瑞典與德國對難民的到來張開雙臂表示歡迎，而一些國家如波蘭與匈牙利則是不願意接納那麼多的難民入境。

European country	supportive attitude towards the Syrian refugees	negative attitude towards the Syrian refugees
Poland		✓
Sweden	✓	
Germany	✓	
Hungary		✓

2. 根據第二段第五句的敘述，一些東歐國家在難民數量激增時，乾脆封閉國界讓難民自生自滅，故 **(B)** 大部分的敘利亞難民在東歐國家順利落腳是錯誤的。

3. 本句上文提到波蘭、匈牙利與波羅的海地區的小國們對於敘利亞難民抱持不甚歡迎的態度，故本句中的他們所指的應該是 **(C)** 波羅的海地區。

4. 根據第二段的敘述，歐盟各國因為自身的「財務能力」不同而採取不同的態度來因應難民危機，富有的國家能夠提供難民「就業機會」而資源較少的國家害怕難民會引發「國民反彈的聲音」，故本題答案為 **(D)** 語言隔閡。

5. 以本文最末兩句提到「敘利亞難民值得全世界的憐憫。世界各國領袖應儘早放下彼此的不同論調，一起拯救生命。」來看，作者應該是認為 **(A)** 敘利亞的難民們急需世界的救援。

refugee n. 難民	civil adj. 國民的	enormous adj. 極大的
flee v. 逃跑	border n. 邊境	battle n. 戰爭
unfortunately adv. 不幸地	political adj. 政治的	development n. 發展
accommodate v. 為…提供住宿	financial adj. 財政的	immigrant n. 移民
worldwide adj. 全世界的	deserve v. 值得	compassion n. 憐憫

李奧納多‧達文西——多才多藝的人

　　李奧納多‧達文西於 1452 年出生於義大利的芬奇 (Vinci) 小鎮。他被公認為文藝復興時期的天才之一。他曾在許多領域工作，包括繪畫、雕刻、數學、工程學和解剖學以及其他學科。為了紀念他在多個領域所取得的成就，達文西經常被稱為「多才多藝的人」(Renaissance Man) 的榜樣。

　　他最著名的身分是畫家。他創作了舉世聞名的肖像〈蒙娜麗莎〉，掛在巴黎羅浮宮中。他還在米蘭著名的壁畫〈最後的晚餐〉中描繪了一個著名的宗教場景。儘管他的發明相較於畫作較不為人所知，但其開創性並不亞於他的藝術作品。他在文藝復興時期就發想了直升機的概念，雖然幾個世紀後才發明了這種製造直升機的技術。他還提出了計算器、太陽能和坦克的設計概念。

　　儘管李奧納多‧達文西的創意大量湧入，但在他一生中幾乎沒有得到實現。他不僅不斷地重做他的計畫，也喜歡對繪畫技術進行災難性的實驗。因此只有少數的作品得以倖存。儘管李奧納多‧達文西的創作還沒有完成，但在未來幾年中，達文西的作品仍然影響著許多藝術家、工程師和科學家。

解析

1. 第三段 ❷ 提到李奧納多‧達文西有個習慣，他經常會重做他的作品，不過卻又鮮少真的完成，並且他喜歡對繪畫技術進行災難性的實驗，所以他留給後世的作品並不多見。

2. 根據第一段最末句的敘述，李奧納多‧達文西之所以被喻為文藝復興時期人物的典範是因為 (A) 他在許多領域都有著卓越成就。

3. 本篇文章第二段主要介紹 (D) 李奧納多‧達文西的創作包括繪畫、直升機、計算機、太陽能與坦克等。

4. 第三段第四句提到李奧納多‧達文西的作品對於後世的影響甚鉅，舉凡藝術界、工程界與科學界等將繼續受到他的啟發，只有 (C) 文學界並未被提及。

5. 本文主要闡述李奧納多‧達文西的生平與創作，因此最有可能出現在 (B) 以文藝復興時期的巨匠為主題的書籍當中。

Renaissance man　多才多藝的人	genius　n.　天才	the Renaissance　n.　文藝復興時期
mathematics　n.　數學	discipline　n.　(大學或學院的) 專業	achievement　n.　成就
portrait　n.　畫像	religious　adj.　宗教的	technology　n.　技術
output　n.　產量	constantly　adv.　不斷地	disastrous　adj.　災難性的
technique　n.　技能	in spite of　儘管	engineer　n.　工程師

咖啡的歷史

　　據說咖啡起源於非洲衣索比亞。傳言一位年輕的牧羊人叫卡爾迪(Kaldi)曾經注意到他的山羊正在吃綠色小灌木叢中的紅色漿果。吃完這些漿果後，山羊高興地跳著舞。卡爾迪決定嘗試一下。他感到精力充沛、頭腦清醒，也興奮地跳舞。從此咖啡的功效被發現了。咖啡隨後從非洲傳播到阿拉伯，在那裡咖啡發展出烘焙的技法，並製成了今天我們所知的飲品。

　　咖啡變成穆斯林文化的重要元素。它被用來幫助穆斯林保持精力充沛，在儀式上能頭腦清醒。 無論他們走到哪裡，咖啡也跟著去到那裡。但是，阿拉伯人小心翼翼地守護著咖啡樹的種植，他們不允許將可繁殖的種子帶出該國。直到17世紀，阿拉伯一直控制著咖啡產業。一個叫做巴巴・布丹(Baba Budan)的穆斯林朝聖者偷偷運送了幾顆咖啡種子到印度，在那裡他建立了一個咖啡農場。不久後，歐洲、印尼和美洲也開始喝咖啡。

　　今日，咖啡在許多文化中佔有特殊地位。世界各地的人們會互約喝咖啡。有些人為了娛樂而喝，而另一些人則不能生活中沒有它。下次當你享受一杯好咖啡的濃郁和苦味時，記得感激卡爾迪和他那些跳舞的山羊。

解析

1. 本文第一段利用非洲衣索比亞的牧羊人故事來闡述咖啡最早的起源，因此本題答案為 (A)。
2. 第二段 ④ 中提到17世紀之前阿拉伯獨佔了咖啡生意。
3. 第二段第五句可得知巴巴・布丹將咖啡種子「偷渡」回印度而非「向阿拉伯的朝聖者買回」，故本題 (D) 的敘述有誤。
4. 根據第一段的敘述，食用咖啡後可讓人精神振奮、思緒清晰，甚至是開心地跳起舞來，只有 (B) 與神對話並未見於文章之中。
5. 本篇文章目的在於 (C) 解釋咖啡的起源，由衣索比亞牧羊人的傳說切入正題並且提到咖啡是如何傳遍全世界，成為廣受喜愛的日常飲品。

Ethiopia n. 衣索比亞（東非國家）	rumor has it 傳聞	shepherd n. 牧羊人
shrub n. 灌木	energetic adj. 充滿活力的	clearheaded adj. 頭腦清晰的
spread v. 傳播	roast v. 烘烤	consume v. 喝
ritual n. 儀式	jealously adv. 小心翼翼地	fertile adj. 肥沃的
pilgrim n. 朝聖者	bitter adj. 苦的	gratefully adv. 感激地

跟墨水漬說再見

　　你可以付超過 300 美元買一支精美昂貴的原子筆，或者花 3 美元買一打平價原子筆。握著一支昂貴的原子筆感覺會很好。它可能鑲著銀或金。而較廉價的原子筆，也許是用塑膠做成的，你可能會覺得它們握起來既輕又不堅固。但是如果談到它們寫起來如何，你會發現其實沒有什麼差別。現今我們用的原子筆，不論它們的價位高低，都具有差不多的給墨結構且寫起來不斷水也不漏墨，但以前的情況並不總是如此。

　　原子筆是由匈牙利作家拉斯洛·比羅 (László Bíró) 在 1930 年代發明的，這發明解決了以往必須分別攜帶鋼筆和墨水的問題。這些最初版本的原子筆筆桿中有裝滿印刷油墨的管子，而圓錐形筆尖裡則裝有一顆小球。當筆在紙上滑動，小球會隨之旋轉並從管中沾附墨水後將墨水留在紙上。但由於印刷油墨既糊又稠，寫的人必須很用力地壓著筆，墨水才會流出來，不然可能會斷墨，如果壓得太用力，墨水常常會大量漏出而把紙染髒。更糟的是，這些筆本身也很容易漏水而毀了作家的衣服。

　　1949 年，派翠克·福勞里 (Patrick J. Frawley) 和弗蘭·西奇 (Fran Seech) 開發出更好的墨水並改善了筆的結構，這些問題得以解決。這種新的墨水流量既平穩也不漏水，而且就算沾到衣服亦能完全洗淨。為了推廣他的新墨水，發明家會在零售商的襯衫上書寫文字，並表示如果墨水洗不乾淨，他願意賠零售商一件襯衫。結果襯衫每次都能洗乾淨，零售商也愛極了這種墨水。在幾年之內，他就賣出了數百萬支這種新筆，而我們現今所使用的原子筆仍沿用相同的基本墨水配方。

解析

1. 本篇文章主旨在於 (B) 介紹原子筆是如何演進成現代書寫流利又不會弄髒紙張或是衣服。

2. 第一段第五句提到 (D) 原子筆不論是昂貴的或是便宜的書寫起來一樣流暢而且毫不費力。

3. 根據第二段 ❸ 的敘述，使用原子筆書寫時，頂端的小球會隨之滾動並且使筆管內沾附於其上的油墨粘附在紙上。

4. 由本文最後一句可得知，現今所使用的原子筆其油墨配方與 1949 年當時所發明的油墨無異，故本題 (C) 的敘述有誤。

5. 本篇全文講述原子筆由 1930 年代後期至 1949 年的變革，因此最有可能出現在 (A) 以科學與生活為主題的雜誌上。

luxury n. 奢侈	ballpoint pen n. 原子筆	plastic n. 塑膠
flimsy adj. 脆弱的	when it comes to 一談到	barely adv. 幾乎沒有
Hungarian adj. 匈牙利的	blot v. 弄髒	leak v. 漏
smoothly adv. 順暢地	promote v. 推銷	retailer n. 零售商
exchange n. 交換；換貨	remove v. 去除	formula n. 配方

未來廚房

　　想像你正在廚房煮菜，你往下看一眼工作臺上數位食譜的下一個步驟，一位名廚說：「現在加進一小撮鹽，然後攪拌。」你跟著做，然後滑動工作臺前進到互動式烹飪課程的下一步。接著你伸手到烤箱中取出正在煮的魚，但是當隔熱手套接觸到盤子時，手套會告訴你：「魚還沒煮好，請再稍待幾分鐘。」這看起來也許像是《星際爭霸戰》某一集的場景，但它其實是麻省理工學院媒體實驗室未來廚房 (CI) 裡的一項計畫。

　　這個由發明家、科學家和研究人員組成的小組將他們的才華投注在一個我們常使用的廚房設備。他們的目的是創造一個智慧型廚房，用任何可能的方式幫助我們。舉例來說，冰箱會記錄哪樣食品快用完了，並自動向商店訂購缺貨的商品；咖啡杯達到適喝的溫度時會告訴你可以享用了；你的刀子在你吃東西之前，會警告你食物裡含有有害的細菌。這些器具結合了感應器及電腦一同運作，讓你的廚房成為一個做起事來更愉快的場所。你將可以烹煮一些你想都沒想過的餐點，而且烤焦爐子裡的東西這種事只會在過去發生。

　　儘管它們提供了便利，但是對於許多人來說，這些智能廚具似乎過於昂貴。以韓國的多媒體冰箱為例。LG 電子公司製造了一款冰箱，可讓你通過內置顯示器觀看電視或上網。多媒體冰箱的價格遠遠高於普通冰箱。並非所有人都能負擔得起。也許在不久的將來，人們就能負擔得起這項廚房科技，會說話的銀製餐具及互動式影像廚師也會跟攪拌機和微波爐一樣普遍。

[解析]

1. 本篇文章主要是介紹 **(B)** 以智能電腦控制的生活家電與廚房用具將為人類的居家生活帶來前所未有的體驗與便利。

2. 本句的上文提到冰箱可以記錄雜貨並且在數量短缺時自動向商店訂購、咖啡杯會在到達最適合品嚐咖啡的溫度時告知使用者，還有刀具會自動判斷食物是否已經產生有害人體的病菌，故本題答案為 **(A)** 廚房器具。

3. 本文最後一句提到這種廚具科技也許在不久的將來就可以在市面上變得普及，讓智能廚具變得像微波爐與攪拌機一樣人人都能買得起，由此可知作者對於智能廚具的未來是 **(D)** 充滿希望的。

4. 根據第二段第四句的敘述，智能咖啡杯會「在到達最適合品嚐咖啡的溫度時告知你」，而智能刀具則是會「在你開動之前警告你食物是否含有有害的病菌」。

smart kitchen appliance	usage
coffee cup	Tell you when it's the right temperature to drink.
knife	Warn you of harmful bacteria in the food before you consume it.

5. 由第二段第四句可得知智能刀具除了切割食物的功能之外，還可以偵測出食物中的有害病菌，故本題 **(C)** 刀具會從智能廚房消失的敘述有誤。

glance　v.　一瞥	counter　n.　工作臺	chef　n.　主廚
pinch　n.　（一）撮	stir　v.　攪拌	interactive　adj.　互動式的
intellectual　adj.　智力的	keep track of　追蹤	shortage　n.　缺乏
bacteria　n.　細菌	combination　n.　結合	sensor　n.　感應器
appliance　n.　用具	monitor　n.　螢幕	affordable　adj.　可負擔的

殖民地的房屋

　　1750 年，北美仍然是一個新世界，這個世界以自然環境為主導。早期移居美國的殖民者居住的環境惡劣，因此這些居民依賴自然的恩賜和自己的辛勤勞動過活。當時，大多數的移民靠務農為生。他們在麻薩諸塞州的普利茅斯殖民地 (Plymouth Colony) 上建造農舍，此為來自英國的殖民者最早定居的地點之一。這些農舍代表昔日的典型建築。

　　由於樹林茂密，早期殖民者的住家都是木製的。典型的住宅有一點五層樓高，並有堅固的木製骨架，外牆也由木材覆蓋建成。家具和廚房工具也用木頭製成。廚房通常是唯一有壁爐的房間，提供烹煮的設備和漫長冬季裡所需的暖氣，而且也是許多家庭活動的中心。殖民地家庭通常很大，所以活動很多，但隱私卻很少。在一樓的其中一側有一間客廳，家人可以在那裡工作及用餐。另一頭則是一間起居室，裡面有最好的家具和父母親的床鋪，也作為招待客人的場所。

　　隨著時光流逝和殖民地人口的增加，農舍及其內部裝潢開始變得更加複雜、更精緻一點。建築風格也隨新殖民者從歐洲各個角落遷入而變得更加多元化。新的習俗和建築品味也隨之帶到了新大陸。隨著移民者向西遷移，在新的國土疆界上建造了各種風格各異的農舍。在我們這個時代裡，那些少數留存了幾世紀的房舍，讓現代美國人回想起他們祖先儉樸的生活。

解析

1. 由第二段第三句可得知許多美國早期殖民地時期的家庭活動都發生在 (C) 廚房，因為廚房是屋子裡唯一有壁爐的地方，可以在漫長的嚴冬裡提供烹煮食物與取暖的功能。
2. 本篇文章的主旨在於 (B) 闡述美國早期殖民地時期的屋舍內部結構與功能。
3. 由第二段的 ❼ 的敘述可以得知，早期的殖民者會在放有最好的家具及父母的床的房間招待客人。
4. 第三段第四句提到當拓荒者前進美國西部時，新開發地區的農舍建造呈現更多樣化的風貌，因此可以得知早期的殖民地時期應該是由美國東部開始，故本題 (D) 的敘述有誤。
5. 由第三段第二句與第三句的敘述可得知當歐洲各地的移民進入美國時，他們也為殖民地時期的建築風格注入自己的傳統與品味等元素，故殖民地時期建築風格的改變與 (B) 移民者的背景不同有關。

colonial	adj. 殖民地的	dominate	v. 主宰	surroundings	n. 周遭環境
settler	n. 殖民者	make one's living by	以⋯維生	found	v. 建立
represent	v. 代表	architecture	n. 建築風格	abundance	n. 豐富
furniture	n. 家具	privacy	n. 隱私權	entertain	v. 款待
construction	n. 建築物	imaginable	adj. 可想像的	ancestor	n. 祖先

谷歌——世界上最好的搜尋引擎

　　你在街上聽到了一首歌。你忘記了歌名，但記住了一些歌詞。你想知道那是哪首歌，但是當你在搜尋引擎的搜尋欄中鍵入歌詞時，你得到了 100 萬個結果。你不知道從哪裡開始。網路就像一片資訊海。沒有有效的搜尋引擎，很難準確地找到所需的內容。幸運的是，谷歌 (Google) 可以在不到 1 秒的時間內引領我們正確的方向。

　　谷歌是一個受歡迎的搜尋引擎，是兩個史丹福大學學生賴瑞・佩吉 (Larry Page) 和索吉・布林 (Sergey Brin) 的智慧結晶。他們所創的谷歌有個前身，叫做搓背 (BackRub)，該系統非常成功，激勵他們設計一個更快、組織更完整的搜尋引擎。1998 年，佩吉和布林將引擎的技術建構完整，並開了他們自己的公司。他們之所以將此新發明稱作「谷歌」，是受到數學術語「googol」的啟發，意思即指數字 1 後面跟著 100 個零。後來這個名詞便象徵 Google 的承諾，會整理網路上找到的無限資訊。

　　谷歌之所以如此成功，是因為它完全致力於搜尋。它的主要功能就是找資料，所以在它的首頁中沒有像廣告或新聞那種會分散注意力的東西。因為谷歌比其他任何同類的搜尋引擎來得更完整也更快速，所以它能帶來真正的驚喜和滿足。當我們在搜尋一篇不知名的文章、一位失聯已久的童年好友、或某種疾病的獨特療法時，通常不會空手而歸。因此，這個世界還是會繼續使用谷歌。

解析

1. 本篇文章主旨在於 (C) 講述網路搜尋引擎——谷歌誕生的過程、命名的意義以及它之所以優於其他搜尋引擎的原因。
2. 由第三段第二句可得知谷歌的首頁上並無任何廣告刊登或是新聞干擾使用者的注意力，故本題 (B) 的敘述有誤。
3. 第二段 ❹ 提到谷歌這個名字乃是源於數學名詞 googol，指的是 1 的後面有 100 個 0，即 10 的 100 次方。
4. 本句上下文提到谷歌的存在純然是為了幫助使用者搜尋資訊，因此不論使用者想尋找什麼樣的主題，谷歌都能讓使用者感到滿意，因此可以得知本題「空手而歸」的意思是 (D) 沒有得到你所想要的內容。
5. 由本文最後一句「這個世界還是會繼續使用谷歌」可得知作者對於谷歌的未來抱持著 (A) 肯定的態度。

search engine　搜尋引擎	memorize　v.　熟記	the Internet　n.　網路
brainchild　n.　智慧結晶	technology　n.　應用技術	mathematical　adj.　數學的
term　n.　術語	commitment　n.　承諾	be devoted to　v.　致力於
primary　adj.　主要的	comprehensive　adj.　廣泛的	genuine　adj.　真正的
end up　以…結束	empty-handed　adj.　空手的	childhood　n.　童年

廣告增加體重

　　小孩會隨著年紀增長而長大，這是十分正常的，但現在他們長大的速度似乎快於年齡增加的速度。監督健康議題的非營利組織「凱瑟家庭基金會」(KFF) 發現，越來越多的美國小孩有過胖的問題。此外，據估計，這些超重的年輕人中的大多數在成年後仍然如此。因此，體重控制是一個長期的問題。通常，大家把兒童時期的肥胖問題歸因於看電視，但看電視使兒童肥胖的原因實在令人相當訝異。

　　人們通常將電視與超重聯繫在一起，認為越多的孩子看電視，他們越不活躍。因此，他們消耗更少的卡路里，進而增加體重。但是，研究表明，兒童期的不運動與超重沒太大的關係。相反，它將責任歸咎於電視食品廣告。近年來，食品公司一直致力於向孩子們宣傳食物，因為平均每個孩子每年看到的廣告超過 40,000 則。難怪小孩們每年在食物上花費數十億美元。而且大部分賣給小孩的食品就是我們所謂的「垃圾食物」：洋芋片、汽水、糖果和速食。食品公司通常用高人氣的角色來販售那些令人發胖的產品：有蜘蛛人麥片以及史瑞克最愛的速食餐廳。小孩很容易受到影響，他們會進而影響父母購買什麼食物。

　　要阻絕孩童肥胖，我們可以做到幾件事情：禁播垃圾食物的廣告、製作有關營養知識的電視訊息、減少每個節目插播的食品廣告數量、為小孩尋找戶外活動，讓他們不能整天看有害的電視廣告。「廣告增加體重」，或許這樣的訊息才應該呈現在電視上。

解析

1. 第二段倒數第二句提到食品公司會 (C) 利用蜘蛛人或是史瑞克這一類高人氣的角色來推銷高熱量的食物。

2. 根據本文最後一段的敘述，要阻遏兒童肥胖症就必須禁止垃圾食品廣告並且減少電視節目播放的食品廣告數量，由此可推知 (B) 電視廣告會鼓勵兒童多吃不健康的食品而變胖。

3. 第一段 ❷ 提到凱瑟家庭基金會是一個專門監督與健康相關議題的非營利組織。

4. 第二段第三句與第四句提到美國兒童日趨肥胖不是因為坐著看電視缺乏運動，而是因為 (D) 電視上的食品廣告。

5. 第一段借用凱瑟家庭基金會所進行的 (B) 調查報告來突顯兒童過重的問題，進而導引出電視與兒童肥胖症之間的關聯性。

age v. 長大	foundation n. 基金會	non-profit adj. 非營利的
monitor v. 監測	issue n. 議題	estimate v. 估算
long-term adj. 長期的	associate v. 把…聯繫在一起	calorie n. 卡路里
inactive adj. 不活動的	consequently adv. 因此	research n. 研究
advertising n. 廣告	ban v. 禁止	exposed to 暴露在…

Unit 26

未來的無人駕駛汽車

　　道路可能會因為超速駕駛、酒後駕車者及開車時使用手機的駕駛員而變得危險。隨著汽車數量的增加，交通堵塞在大城市變得越來越普遍。解決所有這些問題的一種方法可能是把所有駕駛人趕出駕駛座，讓車子自行駕駛。

　　無人駕駛汽車的想法已經存在很長時間了，問題是如何克服技術挑戰。其中一個主要的問題是如何使汽車「看到」道路。一種可能的解決方案是依靠埋在道路中的磁力系統。每輛自動駕駛汽車都將安裝磁力感測器來確認汽車的位置，並將該信息傳輸給控制電腦。另一個可能的方案是電腦視覺系統，不過不難理解惡劣的天氣可能會干擾相機觀察路況的能力。

　　另一個巨大的挑戰是如何讓汽車看見前方的其他車輛和物體後做出反應。兩種可能的解決方案是毫米波雷達及雷射測距器。這兩項技術已在現行的「主動車距控制巡航系統」中使用，這是一種自主啟動的安全系統，可自動調節車輛的速度以保持與前方車輛的安全距離。還可以使用無線通訊技術使汽車之間不斷地「交談」，以確保汽車之間始終保持安全距離。

　　如何將這些有關路況、其他車輛及前方碍礙物的資訊轉換成實際的方向控制、加速和煞車調整，則是接下來的一大挑戰。在無人駕駛汽車中，小型機動控制器將實際取代「駕駛人」。這些機器將從控制電腦接收訊息，並迅速地對方向控制、油門及煞車做適切的調整。在未來的日子裡，無人駕駛汽車有可能被普遍接受與使用，但目前仍有改進的空間。

解析

1. 本篇文章主要介紹 (C) 未來的自動駕駛車、它目前面臨的挑戰與可應用的科學技術。

2. 第三段 ❸ 提到主動車距控制巡航系統是一種主動安全系統，它可以自動調整車速使汽車可以與前車保持安全距離。

3. 根據第二段的敘述，為了要讓自動駕駛車可以「看見」路況，可以在路面上埋設磁力系統並且在車上安裝磁力感測器來偵測車子的位置，或是利用電腦視覺系統來收集路況資訊，因此本題只有 (D) 煞車調整裝置不屬於這個部分。

4. 本文最後一句提到在未來自動駕駛車有可能可以全面上路，由此可推論出 (C) 自動駕駛車早晚有一天會出現在一般道路上。

5. 根據第二段第四句的敘述，能夠透過路面埋設的磁力系統而偵測出車子位置的是車上安裝的磁力感測器而非毫米波雷達，故本題答案為 (A)。

behind the wheel　駕駛（車輛等）	overcome　v.　克服	magnetic　n.　磁鐵
bury　v.　掩埋	detect　v.　探知	vision　n.　視覺
interfere　v.　干涉	millimeter-wave radar　毫米波雷達	laser　n.　雷射
wireless　adj.　無線的	translate　v.　轉換	steer　v.　駕駛
brake　n.　煞車	adjustment　n.　調整	in the blink of an eye　瞬間

Unit 27

虛擬貨幣會佔領世界嗎？

　　人類使用貨幣已有數千年的歷史，但是現在許多人預測未來將是不用現金的。他們認為，鈔票與硬幣將被虛擬貨幣或電子支付取代，例如比特幣 (bitcoin)、Apple Pay 或 PayPal。這些人認為實體的錢會存在，但只會存在於銀行帳戶中。然而，專家認為，未來不會真的是一個只剩空錢包和塑膠卡片的時代。

　　首先，現金仍然是最可靠的購買方式。科學家說，人們對現金的重視程度高於銀行帳戶中的數字。我們似乎很高興能夠看到和觸摸鈔票及硬幣。舊習慣很難改掉，對於大多數的人來說，虛擬貨幣仍然不夠真實。人們更喜歡使用真鈔而不是其他任何選擇。

　　第二，緊急情況下我們總是需要現金。例如，如果因自然災害導致停電，則無法使用線上支付；人們仍然必須採買用品。因此，實在無法想像未來我們將永遠不需要現金。

　　第三，許多人重視自己的隱私。現金是合法的購買方式，銀行無法追蹤。此外，任何現金付款都可以當場完成，因此買家無需擔心債務或貸款利息。更重要的是，省錢專家還建議使用現金有助於避免超支，因為計算紙鈔會提醒我們要更加明智地支出。

　　總而言之，鈔票和硬幣還會繼續被使用。在許多情況下，我們仍然依賴現金更勝於信用卡。

解析

1. 本句上文中提到人類似乎很喜歡可以看得見摸得到鈔票與硬幣的感覺，而虛擬貨幣無法給我們這種真實感，由此可知本句中的「舊習」所指的是 **(D)** 人們喜歡可以實際碰觸硬幣的感覺。

2. 本篇文章主要探討實體貨幣存在的必要性並且主張它擁有虛擬貨幣無法取代的優點，故本題答案為 **(A)**。

3. 本文全篇以實體貨幣與虛擬貨幣的比較為主題，故最有可能出現在 **(C)** 財經網站。

4. 根據本文最後一段提到我們對於鈔票與硬幣的依賴仍然遠大於虛擬貨幣來看，作者對於虛擬貨幣在未來有可能會取代實體貨幣的假設抱持著 **(B)** 不肯定的態度。

5. 本文第三段第二句提到當自然災害引發停電時，人們仍然可以利用實體貨幣購買必需品 (**People can buy things during a power outage.**)；第四段最後一句提到實體貨幣可以幫助人們避免過度支出 (**People can avoid overspending.**)。

digital adj. 數位的	currency n. 貨幣	predict v. 預言
replace v. 取代	empty adj. 空的	old habits die hard 老習慣難改
alternative n. 替代品	disaster n. 災難	available adj. 可用的
purchase n. 購買	value v. 重視	loan n. 貸款
remind v. 提醒	rely on 依賴	circumstance n. 情況

Unit 28

太多抱怨會傷害你

　　你今天有抱怨什麼嗎？根據研究顯示，大多數人在與他人交談時每分鐘至少抱怨一次。為什麼人們抱怨這麼多呢？也許是因為抱怨讓他們心情可以變好一點。簡單來說，人們通常在抱怨後會感覺良好。因此，一旦人們開始抱怨，他們通常會越抱怨越多。不幸的是，其他研究指出，抱怨對我們的健康有害。

　　研究還指出，抱怨可以改變我們的大腦。本質上來說，我們的大腦傾向於盡可能快速和高效地工作。如果你一次又一次地重複做某事，你的大腦將與這項活動建立堅固的聯結。實際上，大腦中的神經元將靠得更近，讓你更有可能從事該特定活動。因此，經常抱怨實際上會「重塑」你的大腦。這意味著你將來可能會抱怨更多，並且可能會開始花更多的時間與其他消極的人在一起。更糟的是，史丹福大學的研究人員發現，經常抱怨會損害大腦解決問題和進行智能思考的能力。另一項研究表明，經常抱怨會導致高血壓甚至肥胖。

　　幸運的是，抱怨的習慣可以改變。一種方法是用感激之情代替抱怨。每當你想抱怨時，只需想一想你會感激的事情即可。研究表明，這可以幫助減輕壓力和焦慮，同時提高能量水平。即使很多人似乎每天都在抱怨，但顯而易見，減少抱怨會帶來多種情感和健康的好處。

解析

1. 第二段第七句中引用了美國史丹福大學進行的研究來證明抱怨會 (D) 損害大腦解決問題及聰明思考的能力。
2. 根據本文上文的敘述，當我們想要抱怨事情時，不妨轉個念想想有什麼事情是我們值得感激的，「這樣」有助於減少壓力與焦慮，由此可得知「這樣」所指的是 (A) 思考我們感激的事。
3. 第一段 ❹ 提到人們經常抱怨可能是因為抱怨讓他們覺得心情可以變好一點。
4. 根據第三段第四句的敘述，人們會因為想到值得感激的事而減輕壓力，故 (D) 經常抱怨的人會覺得比較沒有壓力的敘述有誤。
5. 本篇文章主要探討抱怨對於人體健康的影響與如何改變抱怨的習慣，因此最有可能出現在 (B) 與健康生活相關的雜誌上。

complain v. 抱怨	at least 至少	essentially adv. 本質上
efficiently adv. 效率高地	connection n. 連結	neuron n. 神經元
frequent adj. 頻繁發生的	negative adj. 負面的	intelligently adv. 有才智地
lead to 導致	fortunately adv. 幸運地	gratitude n. 感謝
reduce v. 減少	anxiety n. 焦慮	benefit n. 好處

星星的生與死

　　在宇宙中，沒有永存的事物。就像人類一樣，星星也擁有自己的壽命。科學家認為，星星是由重力壓縮的大量氣體（主要是氫和氦）所形成。氣體會因而產生高溫並引起一系列核反應。通常，星星將繼續發光並發出數百萬年的光。但最終，這顆星星將用盡氫氣作為燃料。當這種情況發生時，星星將開始擴張並成為「紅巨星」。數百萬年後，這顆星星在走向死亡的過程中將崩塌而變成一顆「白矮星」。

　　但是，比我們的太陽大得多的星星會霎那間死去。當它們的氫氣用完時，很可能會產生巨大的爆炸，稱為超新星。超新星的威力可以強大到發出比銀河系中任何其他星星都要明亮的光，並持續短暫的時間。之後，它會迅速黯淡，並在原本的位置留下一個黑洞。

　　時至今日，黑洞仍然是天文學上最大的謎團之一。黑洞會拉入每個離散的原子和接近的粒子。如果有任何東西進入黑洞，它將永遠無法逃脫。科學家們針對黑洞的本質提出了一些理論。有一些研究人員聲稱黑洞就像物質的永久拘留所。但是其他科學家認為，黑洞可能是通往另一個空間的大門。由於黑洞中的重力非常強大，人很可能會被壓碎，變得比自己的影子更扁。也許有一天，科學家將解決黑洞之謎，但可能不會在近代揭開。

解析

1. 第二段 ❷ 提到當星星內部的氫氣燃燒殆盡後便會發生大爆炸即為超新星。
2. 根據第一段的敘述，星星是由大量的氣體聚集而形成，當星星最終燃燒完氫氣後，它會開始擴張成「紅巨星」，歷經數百萬年後，星星就會崩塌變成「白矮星」而逐漸死亡，因此選 **(A)**。
3. 本篇文章主要講述 **(D)** 星星從誕生一直到死亡的各種階段與歷程中會發生的一些天文現象。
4. 第三段第七句提到黑洞中的重力極大，如果有人進入黑洞，那麼他將會被重力壓得比自己的影子還要更扁，由此可知 **(C)** 的敘述有誤。
5. 第一段第六句提到氫氣的作用就是星星內部的燃料，故本題答案選 **(B)**。

span　n.　一段時間	hydrogen　n.　氫氣	gravity　n.　地心引力
nuclear　adj.　核能的	fuel　n.　燃料	collapse　n.　瓦解；崩塌
substantially　adv.　在很大程度上	galaxy　n.　星系	astronomy　n.　天文學
stray　adj.　零星的	atom　n.　原子	particle　n.　粒子
escape　v.　逃離	dimension　n.　空間	crush　v.　壓扁

思維機器的興起

在人與機器的戰鬥中，人類可能會從自己的創造物中學到一些東西。一個名為華森 (Watson) 的人工智慧 (AI) 電腦系統在美國流行的電視益智節目 《危險邊緣》 (*Jeoprady!*) 中，擊敗了兩名有史以來最出色的參賽者。在為期兩天的錦標賽中對抗連續創下 74 場勝利記錄的肯・詹金斯 (Ken Jennings)，以及該節目贏過最多獎金的參賽者布拉德・魯特爾 (Brad Rutter)。華森輕鬆地擊敗了身為人類的競爭對手。這場勝利為電腦的創造者 IBM 贏得了 100 萬美元的獎金，也使人們對華森的存在意義產生更多的思考。

華森實際上是由許多 IBM 的伺服器連結而成，使得整體的系統效能獲得提升。這個「思維機器」使用其專門的軟體，不僅可以理解人類的語音，而且可以用合成的聲音精確地回答問題。當華森被問到問題時，它會迅速搜尋存儲的大量知識，例如字典、文學作品以及維基百科的全文。它每秒可以處理 100 萬本書，並根據在數據庫中找到的 3 個最可能的答案做出回應。

在《危險邊緣》節目中，華森以一個螢幕顯示器作為虛擬化身，跟它的人類競爭對手排在一起。與人類不同的是，華森本體無法離開 IBM，因為沒有電力它就無法啟動。但是，電腦在按下按鈕回答問題的速度上具有巨大的優勢。

輸了之後，肯・詹金斯便在電視螢幕上寫了一條幽默的信息：「我，一個人類，恭賀迎接我們的新電腦霸主。」但是，大多數分析家都認同華森的勝利對人類是有益的。華森的成功代表我們可以構建人工智慧系統來分析複雜的問題並根據複雜的演算流程提出解決方案。這也是一個人們可以用來解決安全、醫療和金融等各個領域問題的技術。

解析

1. 第一段第二句提到華森是人工智慧電腦系統，故本題答案為 **(D)**。
2. 根據第一段 ❹ 的敘述，華森在益智節目中打敗其他實力堅強的對手並抱走 100 萬美元的獎金。
3. 第四段最後一句提到華森的成功代表了 **(B)** 人工智慧系統未來可以應用在多種領域上，分析複雜的問題並且提出可能的解決方案。
4. 第一段第二句提到《危險邊緣》是一個在美國廣受喜愛的電視益智節目，因此 **(A)** 的敘述有誤。
5. 根據第四段第二句與最後一句的敘述，大部分的分析家都認為華森的例子證明了人工智慧系統對於人類有著極大的助益，未來亦可應用於幫助人類解決不同領域的挑戰，由此可知作者對於人工智慧系統的未來抱持著 **(C)** 充滿希望的態度。

versus prep. 以⋯為對手	tournament n. 錦標賽	defeat v. 擊敗
server n. 伺服器	overall adv. 總的（來說）	capacity n. 效能
software n. 軟體	vast adj. 廣大的	literary adj. 文學的
process v. 處理	enormous adj. 極大的	participant n. 參加者
analyst n. 分析者	demonstrate v. 演示	finance n. 金融

別把舊手機丟掉！

　　你的手機在緊急情況下可以挽救你的生命，但到了該換新手機時，你的舊手機可能會危害你和其他人及動物的生命。每年有上百萬人丟棄他們的舊手機。當手機被丟到垃圾堆裡，它們所含有的有毒物質就會很容易汙染我們的環境。

　　手機和其他無線電子產品含有危險的化學物質，例如砷、銅、鉛、鎳和鋅。這些化學物質被認為與癌症、神經系統和生殖系統失調有關。如果這些電子產品被當作廢物燒毀，有害的化學物質將被釋放到空氣中。如果將它們掩埋在垃圾掩埋場中，化學物質將汙染土壤和地下水。這些有害的物質會在環境中殘留很長時間。它們可能會在動物體內累積，對這些動物本身及食用動物的人造成健康危險。

　　為了下一代著想，一個名為 INFORM 的環境研究組織做了一個研究，想找出防止電子產品造成毒性汙染的最佳方法。他們建議製造商應減少這些產品中使用的有毒物質，並提出可永續利用的設計，讓它們可以再利用並具有經濟效益。INFORM 還要求世界各國政府通過法令，鼓勵電子製造商提出更環保的設計。澳洲、日本、美國和歐盟都開始通過相關法令，但即使如此，電子產品要真正環保，還需要很多年。

　　為了保護環境，我們現在所能做的是安全地將我們的舊手機丟棄。將它捐贈給慈善機構、送給可回收利用的團體，或請製造商修理後再次賣出，就是別把它扔進垃圾桶！

解 析

1. 本篇文章主要闡述 (B) 任意拋棄無線電子產品而且缺乏妥善處理的話，會使其釋放出有毒的化學物質，進而造成嚴重的汙染問題。

2. 第二段第一句與第二句提到手機以及其他無線電子產品 (C) 內含有毒物質，而這些有毒物質會引發癌症、神經系統與生殖系統失調。

3. 根據第二段第二句的敘述，手機與其他無線電子產品所含的有毒化學物質，可能會引起癌症、神經系統與生殖系統失調，這其中不包括 (B) 流行性感冒。

4. 根據第二段第四句的敘述，如將廢棄的手機當作垃圾掩埋，則其內含的有毒化學物質將會造成土壤與地下水汙染，故 (A) 將舊的手機直接丟進垃圾並不是可以避免手機汙染環境的可行方法。

5. 第三段 ❶ 提到 INFORM 是一個專門進行環境研究的組織。

toss v. 扔	endanger v. 危害	discard v. 拋棄
pollute v. 汙染	material n. 材料	electronic adj. 電子的
disorder n. 混亂；失調	release v. 釋放	landfill n. 垃圾掩埋場
groundwater n. 地下水	conduct v. 實行	manufacturer n. 製造商
economical adj. 經濟的	environment-friendly adj. 環保的	recondition v. 修理

31

神奇的亞馬遜河

　　亞馬遜河雖然不是世界上最長的河流，卻擁有全世界上最廣大的河流系統——亞馬遜流域。亞馬遜河包含了全世界流入海洋中大約 20% 的水。它也是亞河豚 (Boto)，也被稱為亞馬遜河豚，以及惡名昭彰的食人魚的主要棲息地之一。

　　亞馬遜河也是跨及巴西、委內瑞拉、哥倫比亞、厄瓜多與秘魯十億英畝的亞馬遜雨林的生命原動力。亞馬遜雨林是許多驚人的生物的家園，其中包括世界上最大的蛇和淡水魚。它也被稱為「地球之肺」，因為它提供了將二氧化碳轉換為氧氣所不可或缺的環境。世界上大約有 5% 的二氧化碳會被雨林吸收。數量看起來似乎很少，但影響卻很大。不幸的是，這個數字正在下降當中。

　　儘管國際社會越來越關注環境保護，但亞馬遜雨林卻時時刻刻都因為它的經濟價值而不停地被破壞。在過去的 50 年中，大約 17% 的雨林被摧毀，這給世界各國帶來了悲劇性的後果。

　　在為時已晚之前，世界各地的環保人士正在採取各種措施來拯救這片獨特的森林。大多數人也意識到保護現存雨林的必要性，同時也知道要照顧依賴雨林維生的人們的生活。如果能妥善處理，雨林可以繼續提供全世界許多資源需求。

解 析

1. 第二段 ❶ 提到亞馬遜雨林幅員遼闊，而亞馬遜河沿途流經巴西、委內瑞拉、哥倫比亞、厄瓜多與祕魯等國家。
2. 根據第二段第四句的敘述，亞馬遜雨林的外號是「地球之肺」，因為它能夠 (B) 吸收大量二氧化碳並排放出氧氣。
3. 第三段第一句中提到亞馬遜雨林被摧毀的主因是由於「它」所帶來的利益，故本題答案為 (D) 亞馬遜雨林。
4. 根據第三段第一句的敘述可得知造成亞馬遜雨林受到大規模砍伐與破壞的主因是 (A) 經濟利益。
5. 第四段第一句提到全世界的環保人士正在採取各種措施來保護剩餘的雨林，由此可知雨林並不是取之不盡、用之不竭的再生資源，故本題 (D) 的敘述有誤。

basin　n.　流域	approximately　adv.　大約	pour into　流入
habitat　n.　棲息地	notorious　adj.　惡名昭彰的	piranha　n.　食人魚
convert　v.　轉換	carbon dioxide　n.　二氧化碳	oxygen　n.　氧
concern　n.　關注	profit　n.　利潤	yield　v.　產生
consequence　n.　後果	environmentalist　n.　環保人士	remaining　adj.　剩餘的

洪水和乾旱的成因

　　以經濟損失和死亡人數來看，洪水是世界上最嚴重的自然災害之一。而乾旱更為嚴重。它可能持續數十年，並造成更大的經濟和生命損失。洪水和乾旱似乎有非常不同的成因：洪水是因為水過多，而乾旱是因為水太少。但是，實際上，這些災難的起源通常是相同的。

　　環境保育人士認為，人對土地的濫用通常會增加洪水和乾旱的機會。例如，燒耕的方式會促使土質惡化。燒耕是一種砍伐和燒毀森林以種植農作物的耕作方法。隨著樹木和其他原生植物消失，土壤中的養分將被沖走。更糟糕的是，人們經常把土壤壓實以進行施工，導致土壤變緊且水難以滲透；同樣地，水泥地面也不能吸收珍貴的水。結果，當遇到長時間的乾季時，土地乾涸、作物枯萎和死亡。即使暴風雨帶來強降雨，乾涸的土地也不能夠很好地吸收水分。河流和湖泊將溢出並淹沒貧瘠的土地。

　　儘管自然是造成暴雨或長時間乾旱的動力，但人類的行動往往是洪水和乾旱的根源。如果我們決心防止洪水和乾旱的發生，水和土地的管理至關重要。

解析

1. 本句上文提到水災會奪走許多條人命並且帶來重大的經濟損失，而旱災所造成的影響更甚於水災，因為「它們」可能持續的時間更長，故本題答案為 (A) 旱災。
2. 根據第一段第二句與第三句的敘述，旱災 (B) 帶來的死亡與財損將更甚於水災。
3. 本篇文章主要介紹水災與旱災的起因，因此最有可能出現在 (C) 地理電視節目。
4. 本文於第二段 ❸ 指出所謂的「燒耕」是一種將森林砍伐並加以燒毀來耕種作物的農業方法。
5. 由第二段第三句與第四句可得知當森林與其他原生植物被砍伐燒毀後，土壤中的養分也會在經過雨水沖刷後而消失殆盡，故本題 (C) 的敘述有誤。

drought　n.　乾旱	disaster　n.　災害	in terms of　從…的觀點
economic　adj.　經濟的	degrade　v.　使降低	nutrient　n.　養分
compact　v.　使密實	penetrate　v.　滲入	concrete　n.　水泥
absorb　v.　吸收	rainfall　n.　降雨	overflow　v.　氾濫
barren　adj.　貧瘠的	extended　adj.　延長的	occurrence　n.　發生

天空中的超級月亮

　　你有沒有看過夜晚的天空，以為月亮看起來異常大呢？如果是這樣，你可能已經看過一次超級月亮了。當月球在軌道上運行至與地球之間距離最短時，就會有超級月亮。這時，月亮將變得生動明亮，比平常大出 14%。超級月亮每年大約發生一次，因此人們很少有機會看到它們。

　　有人認為，超級月亮會引起地震和海嘯。事實上，2004 年和 2011 年發生的兩次重大自然災害都發生在超級月亮出現的兩週內。然而，科學家們並沒有發現超級月亮和地震之間有任何直接關聯，它們對潮汐的影響也很小。

　　在 2015 年，慶祝中秋節的人們享受了這個特殊待遇。9 月 27 日至 28 日，在月全蝕的期間出現了一次超級月亮。這讓月亮變成了超級血月，在夜空中非常明顯。為了宣傳這一活動，中國的一家航空公司提供了數百班特殊航班，讓人們能夠更近地看到超級血月。航空公司希望為在節日期間旅行的人們帶來歡樂。那些無法與家人分享月餅的人，至少可以看到這個特殊的月亮並記得這個節日。

　　從 1900 年以來，只有發生過 5 次血月。任何錯過這次超級血月的人將不得不等待以看到下一個。這個令人難以置信的月亮事件要到 2033 年才會再次發生。

解析

1. 第一段先拋出一個問題來吸引讀者注意，爾後再揭曉「超級月亮」事實上是指在軌道上運行時與地球之間距離最短的月亮，因此本題答案選 (A)。
2. 第一段 ❸ 提到超級月亮發生在當月球在軌道上運行至與地球相距最短的時候。
3. 由第二段第一句的敘述「有人認為，超級月亮會引發地震與海嘯」可得知 (B) 有些人認為超級月亮是不祥的。
4. 第二段第三句指出科學家尚未找到超級月亮與地震發生之間的直接證據，而超級月亮對於潮汐也沒什麼影響，故本題 (B) 的敘述有誤。
5. 根據第三段第二句與第三句的敘述，「超級血月」是發生在 (D) 超級月亮月全蝕的時候。

supermoon　n.　超級月亮	abnormally　adv.　異常地	occur　v.　發生
distance　n.　距離	orbit　n.　軌道	vivid　adj.　明亮的
usual　adj.　通常的	tsunami　n.　海嘯	tide　n.　潮汐
lunar eclipse　月蝕	visible　adj.　顯眼的	enable　v.　使能夠
at least　至少	remind　v.　使記起	incredible　adj.　難以置信的

不再有噪音汙染！

　　我們生活在一個充滿各種聲音的世界。然而，當聲音是討厭的、不悅耳的，或是當它們使我們不舒服時，則可以稱為「噪音汙染」。噪音汙染會干擾我們日常活動的正常進行，並讓人的生活品質變差。儘管有些人認為噪音汙染不如水、空氣或土地汙染等其他類型的汙染嚴重，但我們仍應注意並盡一切努力來預防或減少噪音汙染。事實上，政府和人民可以採取許多措施來解決噪音汙染的問題。

　　例如，政府應該通過法律，強制工廠和製造商必須安裝材料，防止聲音散發出來，特別是如果他們有嘈雜的機器。此外，不應允許在住宅區建造工廠。至於經常產生大量噪音的交通轉運站，例如機場、公車站和火車站，政府可以禁止汽車或機車使用嘈雜的喇叭。嘈雜的摩托車和卡車也應該被禁止上路。除此之外，應在道路旁和住宅區種植樹木和其他灌木叢，因為它們有助於吸收聲音。

　　同時，我們還可以自己做一些事情來對抗噪音汙染。一個簡單的方法是在公共場所將智慧手機切換到靜音模式。地毯、窗簾甚至是大書架也可以阻擋家裡的有害噪音。最後，如果情況變得更糟，你終究可以購買一副耳塞或消除噪音的耳機，以派上用場對抗噪音汙染。

　　我們應該盡力擺脫所有類型的汙染。但是，在噪音汙染方面，我們很幸運地可以採取一些簡單的步驟來預防或減少噪音汙染。

解析

1. 第一段 ❷ 提到當聲音是討厭的或是不是悅耳的，亦或是聲音讓我們覺得不舒服時就是「噪音汙染」。
2. 根據第二段第一句的敘述，政府應該通過法律強制工廠與製造業者安裝隔音設備，尤其是如果「他們」使用的是會發出噪音的機器的話，故本題答案選 (C) 工廠。
3. 由第二段最後一句與第三段第三句可得知樹、地毯與大型書櫃都具有阻隔噪音的功效，故本題應勾選 Trees、Rugs、Large bookshelves。
4. 根據第二段第一句、第三句與第四句的敘述可得知本文並沒有提到 (B) 政府可以鼓勵人民居住在鄉間來減少噪音汙染。
5. 本篇文章第三段主要是 (C) 提出一些方法供個人參考來對抗噪音汙染。

pollution n. 汙染	refer to v. 提到	normal adj. 正常的
pay attention to 關注	install v. 安裝	permit v. 允許
residential adj. 居住的	terminal n. 總站（火車、客運等）	alongside adv. 在⋯旁邊
combat v. 與⋯做鬥爭	mode n. 模式	rug n. 小地毯
earphones n. 耳機	handy adj. 有用的	fortunate adj. 幸運的

你也可以過零浪費的生活

塑膠包裝和一次性餐具正在破壞我們的環境。每當我們扔掉紙杯或餐巾紙時，每次使用塑膠叉子和刀子時，都會造成問題。如今，越來越多的人正在改變自己的習慣，並採取一種「零浪費的生活方式」，他們試著不製造任何垃圾。你可以採取以下行動來減少垃圾並拯救我們的星球。

- **改變飲食習慣**：使用可重複利用的餐具，帶自己的刀叉到傾向使用紙和塑膠容器的餐廳用餐。你同時需要記得去咖啡店時要用馬克杯或玻璃杯而不是紙杯。
- **確保你擁有對環境友善的家用產品**：嘗試用衣料碎布代替紙巾。這樣，你將停止用不必要的垃圾填滿垃圾掩埋場。
- **隨時攜帶自己的購物袋**：塑膠袋分解需要長達 1,000 年的時間，對環境非常有害。
- **如果不環保，請不要購買**：你可以透過拒絕購買來說服生產商不要販賣塑膠包裝的水果和蔬菜。你購物時的選擇可能會對超市包裝商品的方式產生重大影響。

最後，不要單單自己努力，帶上你的朋友！如果你能在一個群體中進行一些小的改變，你將會保持動力。即使是生活習慣上最小的改變也能夠使我們的地球變得更乾淨。

解 析

1. 本篇文章主旨在於 (C) 鼓勵人們透過減少生活中不必要的垃圾，一同來保衛我們所居住的地球。
2. 第一段 ❸ 提到所謂的「零浪費的生活方式」就是盡量不要製造任何垃圾。
3. 最後一段的第一句與第二句提到不要自己獨自做垃圾減量的環保工作，如果可以找一群人一起做會更有動力去執行，因此本題答案選 (A) 找朋友一起過著零垃圾的生活方式。
4. 根據最後一段最後一句的敘述「即使是生活習慣上最小的改變也能夠使我們的地球變得更乾淨」可得知 (D) 生活中小小的改變也能夠對地球產生大大的影響。
5. 本篇文章介紹了 4 種每個人都可以實行的生活小改變：自己攜帶餐具、使用對環境友善的家用產品、使用自己的環保購物袋、拒絕購買非環境友善的產品，故本題只有 (C) 隨手關燈沒有在文章中出現。

lead v. 過（某種生活）	disposable adj. 一次性的	destroy v. 毀壞
nowadays adv. 現今	adopt v. 採用	trash n. 垃圾
modify v. 改變	habit n. 習慣	tend v. 傾向
container n. 容器	household n. 家庭	convince v. 說服
wrap v. 包，裹	on board 一同參與	stay motivated 保持動力

保護自然區

保護自然區是一個挑戰。儘管人們喜歡在那裡度過時光，但無論走到哪裡，他們都會留下自己的印記：廢物、垃圾、汙染和其他對野生動植物的破壞。通常，這種傷害是偶然的，但即使像是散步之類的簡單動作也可能會產生很大的影響，因為每個腳步都可能會損害美好的東西。

保護自然區的一種方法，就是建立國家公園和其他保護區，遊客在進入前都需要獲得許可。這讓管理該區域的人員可以在任何時間控制訪客的數量，從而減少訪客造成的損害。收取入場費還有助於支付維護公園和保育工作的費用。

保護自然區的另一種方法是限制人們可以在自然區進行的活動。例如，某些湖泊禁止使用摩托船，因為它可能會造成汙染和不受歡迎的噪音。許多公園不允許人們升火，這種人類的活動經常導致每年有野火的發生。同樣地，許多海濱地區也受到保護，禁止在當地進行工業開發，許多森林也禁止伐木工人的砍伐。

這樣的法律和規則很好，但除非人們遵守這些規則，否則它們將不會起作用。這樣的教育迫切需要。前往荒野的人們需要意識到自然環境很輕易就會受到破壞。這項教育必須盡早開始，對此的責任在於父母、老師和政府。只有人們先學會珍惜所有，才會下定決心來保護。

解析

1. 由本句的上下文可得知 (A) 國家公園與其他保護區的設立，有助於掌控訪客人數，因而減少人為破壞的情況產生。
2. 根據第二段第二句的敘述，國家公園的設立可以減少人為破壞的產生，故本題 (D) 的敘述有誤。
3. 本篇文章主要闡述保護自然生態區域的方式：建立國家公園或保護區、限制人為活動的種類以及教育民眾以提升人們對於自然環境保護意識等，故最有可能出現在 (C) 國家公園的小冊子。
4. 第三段 ❷ 提到由於摩托船會造成汙染以及製造噪音，所以有些湖泊並不許可摩托船的使用。
5. 由第三段所舉出的兩個例子：有些湖泊禁止使用摩托船與許多公園明令禁止民眾升火可得知 (C) 人類的活動有時候會對自然造成巨大的損害。

preserve v. 保護	challenge n. 挑戰	wildlife n. 野生動植物
accidental adj. 意外的	impact n. 影響	risk n. 危險
establish v. 建立	permission n. 許可	manage v. 管理
decrease v. 減少	conservation n. 保育	industrial adj. 工業的
desperately adv. 非常	wilderness n. 荒野	responsibility n. 責任

超級雜草的崛起

　　20 年前，美國的農業公司引進了新的農作物以增加收成。他們改變了黃豆、棉花、玉米和甘蔗等較重要的農作物的基因。這些特殊的農作物被設計來抵抗化學公司開發用來斬除雜草的強大化學毒物。這些公司認為，他們已經開始了一場農業革命，可以讓農民和消費者受益幾個世紀。在這些巨大的農場上，雜草將不再阻礙農作物的生長。人類似乎已經征服了自然，並戰勝了雜草。

　　然而，在種植這些無雜草作物的農田上，開始出現一些令人不安的現象。藉由這種方式干擾自然，農民似乎實際上引發雜草的自然演進。一些倖存的雜草被發現自然而然地出現可以抵抗毒物的基因。這些植物繁殖後不久，許多雜草對這種化學物質產生了抗藥性。

　　如今的情況非常令人震驚。據說，美國東南部有超過 90% 的棉花和大豆田已經無法阻止頑強雜草的蔓延。這些公司必須花更多的錢用機器或雇用工人來清除雜草。因此，土地的生產和盈利能力正在下降。許多農場正在使用更強大的毒藥殺死雜草，但這將繼續產生會對化學物質有抵抗力的雜草。此外，這些化學物質與農場工人之間的癌症有關，風也將毒物帶給當地居民。

　　超級雜草的興起似乎表明了一件事，使用這些方法的農業公司正在與這最熟悉的宿敵打一場沒有勝算的仗。

解析

1. 第一段第二句提到美國的農業公司將黃豆、棉花、玉米與甘蔗的基因改變使其能夠抵抗除草劑，因而造成了本文中超級雜草的誕生，故本題只有 (D) 香蕉未被提及。
2. 第二段第一句與第二句提到農業公司引進了不會長雜草的農作物，因而使得農作物周圍雜草的基因產生了自然演進的改變，故本題答案為 (B)。
3. 第二段 ❸ 提到超級雜草的特徵就是它們自然而然地出現可以抵抗毒物的基因。
4. 根據第三段第三句與第五句的敘述，農業公司會雇用勞工以人力或是機器來拔除超級雜草而農夫則是嘗試以更強的農藥來殺死它們，故本題 (C) 放一把火把它們燒成灰燼並未在文中出現。
5. 由最後一段作者認為無法想出新招的農業公司在對付雜草這個宿敵上肯定是吃敗仗來看，作者抱持的是 (A) 悲觀的態度。

boost v. 提高	alter v. 改變	sugar cane n. 甘蔗
weed n. 雜草	revolution n. 革命	mankind n. 人類
conquer v. 征服	disturb v. 干擾	phenomenon n. 現象
breed v. 交配繁殖	situation n. 情況	productive adj. 多產的
profitable adj. 有益的	resistance n. 抵抗	indicate v. 顯示

氣候變遷與我們的心理健康

　　氣候變遷在現今社會是一個熱門的話題。我們星球的溫度在上升,引起了連鎖的反應。極地冰帽正在融化,海平面上升將使許多沿海城市陷入水中。

　　在未來的幾十年中,隨著氣候的變遷,地球上的生活將產生很大的變化。所有科學理論都表明生活將會變得更加艱難。此外,社會科學家認為,由於資源有限,我們的星球將變得充滿更多衝突。不僅我們的身體健康受到威脅,我們的心理健康也處於危險當中。由於氣候變化,許多年輕人非常擔心未來充斥著洪水、汙染和食物短缺。有些心理學家稱這種現象為「生態焦慮」。有這種情況的人對未來有著非常悲觀的態度,他們的消極想法常常使他們不快樂。

　　我們都知道,下一代將不得不應對極端的氣候條件。同樣顯而易見的是,將來生態焦慮之類的心理健康問題將會越來越多。為了減少對未來的擔憂,心理學家建議我們應該採取行動應對這些問題,而不要太擔心。成為一名環保主義者,隨時了解環保相關的議題並且教育他人,也會讓你成為一個務實的人。

解 析

1. 根據第一段第三句與第二段第五句的敘述可得知氣候變遷可能會造成海平面上升、水災與被淹沒的城市等連鎖反應,故本題只有 **(B)** 更多環保尖兵並未提及。
2. 第二段 ❺ 提到受到氣候變遷的影響,年輕人最擔憂的是未來會有水患頻繁、嚴重汙染與食物短缺的現象發生。
3. 本文的第二段主要是談到 **(D)** 氣候變遷不只是影響了人們的居住環境,對於人們的心理層面亦有巨大的衝擊,使得不少年輕人對於未來產生焦慮感。
4. 根據本句上文的敘述,如果要降低對未來的焦慮,最好的方式就是採取行動,因而本句中也提到當環保主義者、了解環保相關的議題並且教育他人等行為都是 **(D)** 主動且務實的作法。
5. 本篇文章主旨在於探討氣候變遷如何影響人們的心理健康並且提出因應之道,故最有可能出現在 **(A)** 地理雜誌上。

climate change　n.　氣候變遷	mental　adj.　心理的	temperature　n.　溫度
chain　n.　一連串	the polar ice caps　極地冰帽	melt　v.　融化
scientific　adj.　科學的	theory　n.　理論	not only...(but) also　不但…而且
eco-anxiety　生態焦慮	pessimistic　adj.　悲觀的	prevent...from　防止…
on the rise　在增長	activist　n.　行動主義者	have both feet on the ground　腳踏實地

對抗糧食浪費

　　你可能沒有意識到，但糧食浪費是一個全球性的問題。每年，有幾百萬噸的食物在端上餐桌前就被扔進垃圾桶裡。作為消費者，我們希望我們的食品看起來有吸引力。因此，我們扔掉了夠新鮮的但樣貌不佳的食物。整個食品生產鏈都這麼做。對於生產者來說，他們傾向於丟棄醜陋的水果和蔬菜，因為運輸可能無法販售的物品比丟棄它們要花費更多成本。然後，整個食品供應鏈、超級市場及飯店也重複相同的行為。

　　好消息是，全球許多公司都在與食物浪費進行對抗。例如，英國的應用程式 Olio 每天蒐集大量餐廳和個人不再需要或不想要的食物。這些食物仍然新鮮且可以吃。該應用程式的用戶可以免費領取他人不需要的食物。這樣，食物就能送給珍惜它的人，而不是扔進了垃圾桶。

　　在世界的另一端，加拿大慈善機構「第二收穫」(Second Harvest) 建立了一家食物銀行。這家食物銀行就像其他任何有新鮮食品的雜貨店一樣。但是，這裡堆滿了超市捐贈的食物，因為超市丟棄了幾天之內沒有被售出的食物。

　　總而言之，有數百萬人在飢餓之中，但仍然有食物浪費的情形。這可能會讓你感到煩惱，但這是一個可悲的事實。而且，這種行為對環境有害。我們在生產食物上付出了很多的努力，最後卻扔掉了上噸重的食物。食物浪費是一個全球性問題，但是許多人正在努力與之抗爭並找到有效的解決方案。

解析

1. 第一段 ❻ 提到促使食物生產者將醜陋的水果丟棄是因為運輸它們更花成本。
2. 本句上文提到因為消費者不愛購買外表有缺陷的食物，所以食品的生產者寧願直接丟棄賣相不好的蔬果，因此所有的食物供應商與餐飲業者都是遵循這個作法，故本題答案選 (B)。
3. 根據第二段第四句的敘述，Olio 的用戶可以免費領取被餐廳或是個人淘汰掉的新鮮但樣貌不佳的蔬果，故本題 (D) 的敘述有誤。
4. 本篇文章於第一段中提出糧食浪費的問題與起因並於第二段與第三段中提出解決方法，故本題答案為 (C)。
5. 加拿大慈善組織「第二收穫」機構創立了食物銀行來幫助解決糧食浪費的問題，由此可以推知 (A) 其創辦人關心糧食浪費的議題。

aware adj. 意識到的	million n. 百萬	ton n. 公噸
attractive adj. 誘人的	production n. 生產	behavior n. 行為
considerable adj. 相當大的	individual n. 個人	appreciate v. 珍惜
charity n. 慈善機構	grocery store n. 雜貨店	donate v. 捐贈
in conclusion 最後	harmful adj. 有害的	effective adj. 有效的

全球肥胖

　　「全球肥胖」(globesity) 這個新詞，是「全球的」(global) 與「肥胖」(obesity) 這兩個英文字的簡稱，用來描述全球成長最迅速的健康問題。根據世界衛生組織 (WHO) 的數據，自 1975 年以來，全球肥胖的人數幾乎增加了 2 倍；到目前為止，已有超過 6.5 億人過重。這些人罹患糖尿病、心臟病和某些癌症的機率較高。國際肥胖專案小組 (IOTF) 要求世界各國領袖幫助傳播必須多吃纖維、少吃糖和脂肪的資訊。此外，還需要進行充分的運動。

　　許多專家將全球體重增加的問題歸因於生活作息的改變。研究顯示，60% 的人體重增加，是因為缺乏運動。越來越多人長時間坐在辦公桌。我們開車、搭公車或火車去上班，而不走路或騎腳踏車。一天結束後，我們回到家裡，因為過於疲憊而懶得準備一分健康的餐點，所以我們就隨便買了速食或充滿脂肪和糖的簡便食品來取代。晚餐過後，我們就坐在沙發上看整晚電視。日復一日過著這樣的生活很難想像何謂健康的生活。

　　那麼，到底有什麼解決方法呢？專家們建議我們食用全穀食品與新鮮蔬果，因為它們可以幫助消化。堅果及瘦肉對我們的身體也是不可或缺的，因為它們提供了良好的脂肪和蛋白質。當然我們也需要多做運動。如果每天能花 20 分鐘走路，就可幫助我們變得更健康。

解　析

1. 第一段 ❶ 提到「全球肥胖」是全世界目前成長最迅速的健康問題。
2. 根據第一段第三句的敘述，過重者容易罹患糖尿病、心臟病與癌症，故本題只有 **(B)** 失眠症未被提及。
3. 本篇文章在第一段中借用 **(A)** 世界衛生組織所公告的數據來突顯出全球肥胖的嚴重性。
4. 第二段第三句與第五句提到我們因為工時太長而感到過度疲勞，所以沒有多餘的力氣在下班後準備一頓營養均衡又豐富的晚餐，故本題 **(A)** 的敘述有誤。
5. 第二段第一句提到許多專家認為全球肥胖與生活作息有關，故本題答案為 **(B)**。

short adj. （名字）簡稱的	obesity n. 肥胖	triple v. （使）增加兩倍
overweight adj. 肥胖的	diabetes n. 糖尿病	fiber n. 纖維
adequate adj. 足夠的	necessary adj. 必需的	blame v. 責怪
lack of sth. 沒有…	convenience food n. 簡便食物	the rest 剩餘的部分
routine n. 慣例	wholegrain adj. 全穀物的	protein n. 蛋白質

小小一口，大大問題

　　吸菸是肺癌的主要危險因素。菸草的煙中含有數千種化學物質，其中包括了 60 種以上的已知致癌物質。人們通常把吸菸跟男性聯想在一起，認為因肺癌死亡的人大部分都是男性。然而，最近的報告顯示，吸菸的女性人數迅速增加，而女性患肺癌的機率高於男性。

　　研究顯示菸草對不同的性別有不同的影響。相較於男性，如果女性暴露在相同濃度的煙中，更容易在年輕的時候誘發肺癌。據統計，每年女性肺癌的死亡率比乳癌高，其中有 20% 的婦女並非吸菸者！女性也更可能罹患小細胞癌，這種肺癌擴散迅速。雌激素（女性荷爾蒙）亦被認為是刺激肺癌細胞成長的因素之一。即使抽菸對身體有害，在美國每 5 位女性中仍有 1 位抽菸。很多女性就是無法理解當她們抽菸時，所冒的風險有多大。

　　雖然醫療不斷的進步，肺癌患者的 5 年存活率僅有 19%。預防肺癌的最佳方法簡單來說就是戒菸（或者最好永遠不要開始抽菸）。罹患肺癌的風險會隨著抽菸的量、時間長短及抽菸的頻率而增加。女性若戒菸會大大降低提早死亡的機率，所以不論在任何年齡，戒菸都是有益的。

　　最近，全世界的人們開始更加關注女性的吸菸問題。反對菸草公司的積極抗爭進行著。我們必須做出行動吸引大眾關心吸菸對女性健康的影響，同時反對菸草產業鎖定女性為客群的策略來盡一分抗癌的心力。

解 析

1. 本篇文章的主旨在於 (A) 闡述女性吸菸的比例日漸增加而吸菸為女性帶來的健康隱憂更甚於男性。
2. 根據第二段倒數第二句的敘述，在美國每 5 名女性中就有 1 人吸菸，故美國女性吸菸的比例佔總人口的 (D) 20%。
3. 第二段第三句提到每年女性的肺癌死亡人數高於乳癌，故本題 (A) 的敘述有誤
4. 本文內容與女性吸菸與其健康議題有關，故最有可能出現在 (B) 醫學報導之中。
5. 第三段 ❷ 提到預防肺癌最好的辦法就是戒菸或是從不吸菸。

puff n. 一小口（煙霧）	tobacco n. 菸草	substance n. 物質
gender n. 性別	statistics n. 統計數據	breast cancer 乳癌
hormone n. 荷爾蒙	stimulate v. 激發	comprehend v. 充分理解
quantity n. 數量	duration n. 持續時間	prematurely adv. 過早地
beneficial adj. 有益的	campaign n. 活動	launch v. 發起

背痛之苦

　　如果你有背痛的問題，你並不孤單。背痛是人類最常見的抱怨之一，它發作起來可是不分年齡、社經背景或種族的藩籬。幾乎 80% 的人口都有可能或已經遭遇過某種形式的背痛。在我們的社會裡，背痛已經成為普遍性的流行病，也是人們尋求醫療照顧的一項主因。

　　造成背痛的原因有很多，像肌肉扭傷或痙攣等可能是由於粗重的勞動工作、不自然的彎腰或扭轉、姿勢不良等等所引起。整體來說，現代人靜態的工作性質及生活方式是罹患背痛的主因。這種疾病的症狀從惱人的持續性小痛到極度劇烈的疼痛都有，而且還可能會導致工作效率低落，甚至是殘疾。在美國，背痛患者每年花在醫學檢查及治療上的金額就超過了 1,000 億美元。

　　如果痛感較輕微，適當的休息加上適當的運動和藥物治療通常是主要的療法。使用冰敷袋或熱水瓶貼在背上也可能幫助減輕疼痛。在大多數的病例中，治療背痛不需要動手術，通常急性背痛在數日或數週後就會自動復原，然而如果使用這些簡便的療法後，疼痛仍持續一段時間，手術可能會是最有效的解決方案。

　　會不會得到背痛要看你在工作及在家中時如何使用背部。如果你想要保持背部的健康，那麼隨時動動你的背。當你靜止不動時，背部有良好的支撐也很重要。另外，務必保持姿勢正確、開始持續性的居家運動計畫、並以合理的飲食維持健康體重，才可以讓背痛遠離你。

解析

1. 本句上下文的敘述中提到全球有 80% 的人口都曾經有過背痛的經驗，而背痛也是人們最常遭遇的身體不適症狀之一，故可得知 (B) 背痛的毛病不分年齡、社經背景或是種族。

2. 由第二段第二句可得知粗重的體力勞動、姿勢不良或是不自然的彎腰扭轉都會加重背痛的程度，故本題只有 (D) 合理的飲食未被提及。

3. 第二段 ❺ 提到深受背痛之苦的美國人每年要花 1,000 億美元在背痛的醫學檢查與治療上。

4. 第三段第四句提到 (C) 背痛常常在數日或是數週後會自動消失，因此並不需要手術治療。

5. 由第四段最後一句可得知 (A) 保持居家運動的習慣可以預防背痛的發生。

seek v. 尋求	strain n. 扭傷	awkward adj. （肢體）不自然的
posture n. 姿勢	symptom n. 症狀	annoying adj. 惱人的
disability n. 殘疾	medication n. 藥物	examination n. 檢查
therapy n. 治療	mild adj. 輕微的	ease v. 減輕
surgery n. 外科手術	acute adj. 急性的	persistent adj. 堅持的

加糖嗎？

研究指出嬰兒一出生就偏好甜味勝過其他味覺。對很多人而言，這樣的偏好會跟著我們一生。然而，我們飲食中的甜食卻可能或多或少對我們的身體造成傷害。糖分除了會降低之後吃正餐的食慾跟造成蛀牙之外，還會讓我們難以控制體重。人們已試著少吃甜食，但還是很難完全放棄它。如果我們想要享受有甜味的食物，而不攝取糖分，那麼代糖就是一種選擇。可是有一些關於代糖的疑慮可能會讓我們感到疑惑，到底它們對身體是好還是不好？

第一個關於代糖常見的疑慮是安全問題。糖精和阿斯巴甜是兩種最普遍的代糖，它們常用在口香糖跟冰淇淋這類的產品中。由於有研究根據動物實驗證明糖精跟癌症有關連，代糖飽受反對者批評。另一方面，代糖的支持者（尤其是需要減少糖攝取量的糖尿病患者）宣稱少量攝取代糖不會造成危害。雖然不能確定這些添加物會不會導致人類得到癌症，但只要吃的不是天然的食物，我們都應該要小心。

第二個關於代糖的疑慮是有些人相信人工增甜劑可以幫助減肥。事實上，沒有可靠的證據顯示有這樣的作用。換言之，代糖並不是可以讓身上幾磅肉消失的神奇食物，代糖只對大致的體重控管有幫助，還需要包含運動和健康的飲食才可以。

代糖不見得會危及我們的健康，但是也不會有什麼好處。如果想要減重，最好的方法還是得加強自制力，選擇較健康的食物而減少飲食中攝取過多的糖分。

解析

1. 由第一段第一句可得知 (A) 嬰兒天生就偏愛甜味。
2. 第一段 ❹ 提到攝取糖分可能會破壞正餐的食慾、造成蛀牙，還會讓我們體重上升。
3. 本句的上文提到糖精與阿斯巴甜這兩種最常見的代糖，而本句中的糖尿病患者因為必須減少糖分的攝取，所以主張少量的使用 (B) 糖精與阿斯巴甜不會危害到人體健康。
4. 根據第二段第一句、第二句與第四句的敘述，阿斯巴甜既是代糖也是人工甜味劑，故本題只有 (D) 甜食與其他三者不同。
5. 由第四段第二句可得知想要成功減重就必須減少飲食中糖分的過度攝取並且改吃營養健康的食物，故本題 (A) 的敘述有誤。

preference n. 偏愛	sweetness n. 甜味	apart from 除了
spoil v. 破壞	decay v. 腐蝕	substitute n. 代替物
option n. 選擇	ingredient n. 成分	consumption n. 消耗量
calories n. 卡路里	reliable adj. 可信賴的	evidence n. 證據
necessarily adv. 不可避免地	strengthen v. 增強	excessive adj. 過多的

克服疲勞

　　疲勞是人感到疲累、倦怠的狀況。大部分的人都曾因睡眠不足或疾病而感到疲勞。

　　下列是一些導致疲勞的例子：壓力、荷爾蒙失調、憂鬱症、心、肺、血液疾病及癌症。缺乏運動及不佳的身體狀況也會導致疲勞。現在大部分的工作都仰賴電腦，人們花更多時間在電腦前打字與使用滑鼠。因此很多人因為卡路里消耗不足而肌肉退化、變胖。有時候就算沒什麼明顯的原因，人也會感到疲勞，所以最重要的是要有大量的睡眠來給你的身體充電。所以當爸媽週末試圖要把你叫醒時，你可以告訴他們你需要休息來防止疲勞！

　　除了得到足夠的休息之外，均衡飲食也是很重要的。適當的飲食習慣是防止疲勞最簡單的方法之一，因為我們的身體需要能量進行消化、血液循環、排除廢物等重要的機能。另一個防止疲勞的方法就是規律地運動。像是舉重、走路、有氧舞蹈等運動可以鍛鍊肌肉並降低體脂肪。多點肌肉、少點脂肪會讓你更有精神。

解析

1. 由第一段第二句與第二段第一句可得知缺乏睡眠、壓力、荷爾蒙失調、憂鬱症、心、肺與血液疾病、癌症等都會引發疲勞的現象，故本題只有 **(B)** 宿醉未被提及。

2. 由本句的下文可得知電腦文書工作讓人花費更多時間在打字與使用滑鼠上，這種消耗熱量低的工作容易讓人 **(A)** 逐漸流失肌肉並且變胖。

3. 根據第二段第六句的敘述，有時候人們會毫無來由地感到疲倦，此時只要獲得充足的睡眠就可以幫身體充電恢復精神，故本題 **(C)** 的敘述有誤。

4. 由第二段第六句、第三段第一與第三句，可知本題應勾選 Get more sleep、Take regular exercise、Eat a balanced diet。

5. 第三段 ❷ 提到身體需要適合的飲食來提供各種重要機能所需的能量，如消化、血液循環與排除廢物等。

fatigue	n. 疲勞	condition	n. 狀態	weary	adj. 極為疲勞的
imbalance	n. 失調	physical	adj. 身體的	as well	也
computer-based	adj. 以電腦為主的	obvious	adj. 明顯的	wake sb. up	叫醒（某人）
aside from	除了⋯之外	balanced	adj. 均衡的	diet	n. 飲食
circulation	n. （血液）循環	removal	n. 除去	aerobics	n. 有氧運動

發燒可以幫助我們對抗疾病

　　我們似乎偶爾都會散發一點熱度。運動、舞蹈、吃飯、生氣、甚至是戀愛等活動都使我們的體溫上升，但這些都是良性的發熱，並不需要吃退燒藥。不幸的是，我們所熟悉的「真正」的發燒，完全是另一回事。沒人喜歡「真正」的發燒所導致的熱度與頭痛。雖然發燒很難受，不過或許我們該學會理解發燒的好處了。

　　我們正常體溫應該在 37°C 左右。當體溫超過 37.5°C 時，我們可能發燒了。我們很自然地會把發燒與臥病在床、關節酸痛、打冷顫聯想在一起。事實上，發燒是生病的徵兆。小至耳朵發炎、大至癌症都會讓我們的體溫攀升。這是因為每當細菌或病毒入侵身體時，身體都會以熱度殺死它們。發燒也讓身體的免疫系統更有效率地運作。一旦體溫上升，身體就釋出更多的白血球及抗體。因此發燒是一種身體的防衛機制。

　　發燒時我們應該怎麼辦？發燒時我們最好洗溫水澡、增加水分的攝取、好好休息。記住：發燒是身體用來警告我們細菌或病毒入侵的一種方式。然而，你的身體狀況若沒有好轉的話，看醫生可能才是最好的解決辦法。

解析

1. 由第一段第二句可得知運動、跳舞、吃飯、生氣或甚至是戀愛都會使人體體溫略為升高，故本題只有 (B) 肺病未被提及。
2. 由本句的敘述：當細菌或是病毒入侵身體時，「它」便會以升高體溫的方式來殺死這些不速之客可得知「它」所指的是 (D) 人體。
3. 第二段 ❷ 提到當人體的體溫超過攝氏 37.5°C 時就是發燒了。
4. 由第二段第三句與第九句可得知 (C) 雖然發燒讓人很不舒服，但是它是人體重要的防衛機制。
5. 根據第二段第五句的敘述，罹癌者體溫會上升而非下降，故本題 (D) 的敘述有誤。

disease　n.　疾病	familiar with　對⋯熟悉	despite　prep.　儘管
discomfort　n.　不適	hover　v.　徘徊	bed-ridden　adj.　臥床不起的
joint　n.　關節	signal　n.　跡象	infection　n.　感染
virus　n.　病毒	invade　v.　入侵	immune system　n.　免疫系統
antibody　n.　抗體	defense mechanism　n.　防衛表現	consult　v.　諮詢

我們生氣時發生什麼事？

　　我們都知道生氣的人看起來是什麼樣子——張大眼、紅著臉、手顫抖、頸部與太陽穴的血管賁張。但為什麼生氣的人看起來會這樣呢？要回答這個問題，我們必須回溯到數千年前的人類歷史，當人類遇到野獸、大自然及同類之間相互威脅時的時期。對早期人類而言，生氣通常就表示身體遇上危險了。科學家將這整套身體反應稱為「戰逃反射」，憤怒可以迫使我們早期的祖先立即做出攸關生死的決定。幸好，對我們大部分的人而言，這些讓我們祖先生氣的危險因素已不復存在。但即使觸發怒火的因素改變了，身體對生氣的反應並沒有因此而改變。

　　我們生氣時，身體會分泌一種名為腎上腺素的天然化學物質。當腎上腺素進入血液時，就會讓人產生興奮感，使反射動作變敏銳，並加速我們的反應時間。當這種情況發生時，我們的心跳就會由靜止心率每分鐘約 80 下的速度加速到每分鐘約 180 下。除此之外，我們的血壓和體溫都會上升。呼吸變快且變淺。肌肉會緊繃，因為有更多血液流入肌肉中並準備行動。眼睛的瞳孔放大，好讓更多光線進入，使視力變得更為銳利。身體快速燃燒卡路里，以致於我們常在生氣者身上看到的顫抖動作。

　　經過這麼久，我們的身體仍將生氣與危險畫上等號。身體對於危機的反應並未改變。每當我們發怒或處於威脅當中，身體仍會做好激烈運動的準備，就跟祖先們一樣。

解 析

1. 本篇文章的第二段主旨在於 (B) 描述人體在生氣時產生的各種變化，包括心跳加速、血壓與體溫升高、肌肉緊繃、反應時間變短及瞳孔放大等。
2. 第二段 ❶ 提到當我們生氣時，身體會自動分泌腎上腺素。
3. 由第二段第四句的敘述可得知 (C) 當人們生氣時，血壓與體溫都會上升。
4. 由第二段第六句可得知在我們生氣時，流入肌肉的血液量會增加，故本題 (D) 的敘述有誤。
5. 根據第三段最後一句的敘述，(D) 當我們面臨威脅或是生氣時，我們體內的變化會像我們的祖先一般。

vein n. 靜脈	bulge v. 鼓起	response n. 反應
fight-or-flight 或戰或退	immediate adj. 立即的	survival n. 生存
trigger n. 觸發…的原因	adrenaline n. 腎上腺素	bloodstream n. 血液
sharpen v. 提高；使敏銳	reflex n. 反射作用	tense v. 變得僵直
tissue n. 組織	equate v. 使相等	intense adj. 強烈的

保持輸血供給安全

　　如果你出了嚴重的意外，可能需要輸血保命。這是一個醫療過程，血液被注射到病人的身體，以提供缺失的部分，如紅血球或白血球。但你曾顧慮過你在手術時輸的血是否安全嗎？從現在開始，你應該了解更多關於輸血供給安全所做的措施，因為這往往都是攸關生死。

　　為了確保提供緊急醫療使用的血液安全無虞，紅十字會與紅新月會國際聯合會及其他世界各地的類似組織都很努力。有 3 個主要的步驟來確保血液的乾淨與可用性。

　　首先是僅接受自願無償捐血者的血液，絕不接受賣血者的血。無償的捐血者比較願意誠實回答一連串的篩檢問題，原因是這些人不會為了錢而捐贈血液，因此說謊沒有好處。健康篩檢的問題如「你有服用什麼藥物嗎？」、「你有行使安全性行為嗎？」等是杜絕汙染血液的第一道防線。如果自願捐血者的答案顯示他們可能帶有疾病，或當下似乎不夠健康而無法捐血，他們就會被拒絕。

　　一旦從健康的自願捐血者取得血液後，技術人員會檢查血液是否帶有某些疾病，包括愛滋病、肝炎、梅毒。只有完全通過實驗室測試的血液才會再做進一步的處理。接下來，血液會送入過濾器中移除白血球，因為白血球常常造成輸血病人的排斥反應。

　　最後，在經過所有程序後，技術人員將血液貼上標籤並儲存起來。為了確保血液不受汙染並可安全使用，他們將血液存放在安全的地方直到需要輸血為止。收集與分送血液的組織相當重視安全需求。紅十字會表示：「我們的血液供給再安全不過了。」所以如果你需要輸血，你可以相信其安全性。

解析

1. 本篇文章的主旨在於藉由詳述捐助者的血液如何受到嚴格的篩檢以及如何進行保存來 (C) 讓讀者安心使用血庫中的血液。
2. 第三段 ❺ 提到捐血者會被要求回答服用哪些藥物與採取哪些措施來保障自己的安全性行為等問題。
3. 由第三段、第四段與第五段的敘述可得知捐助者的血液是經過採集、化驗、過濾掉白血球後再行貼標籤與儲放等過程，故此題選 (A)。
4. 根據第三段第六句可得知 (D) 如果捐助者貌似不健康或是患有某種疾病就無法捐血。
5. 本句上文中提到經過層層把關處理後的血液最後會交到技術人員的手上，由他們來進行貼標籤與儲放的動作，由此可推知本句中的他們所指的是 (C) 技術人員。

blood transfusion n. 輸血	inject v. 注射	component n. 成分
assure v. 向…保證	volunteer n. 自願者	donor n. 捐血者
screening n. 篩檢	reject v. 拒絕接受	hepatitis n. 肝炎
syphilis n. 梅毒	lab n. 實驗室	filter n. 過濾器
technician n. 技術員	secure adj. 安全的	distribute v. 分發

你該害怕你吃的食物嗎？

　　人類科技進步神速，但並非永不出錯。人類在改良食物的生產與品質上的努力，已經引起食物安全性的極大爭議。有人創造了一個新詞來形容大眾對可能有害食物的感覺：食物恐懼。

　　「食物恐懼」一詞原本是指對基因改造 (GM) 食物安全性的疑慮。雖然相同物種間的選拔育種已經施行數世紀之久，但科學家現在已經可以把基因由某一物種移植到另一物種上。例如：將魚類不會結凍的基因移植到蔬菜上，讓農夫能夠早點栽種以提高獲利。然而，有關基因改造食物對人體長期影響的研究卻很少。若某食物內能引起過敏的基因出現在另一個物種，結果引起了食用者嚴重的過敏反應怎麼辦？或者是，如果基因改造食物對抗生素產生抗藥性或變成有毒的食物怎麼辦？

　　像殺蟲劑等化學藥品引發了疑慮。用來防止農作物病蟲害的化學物質在收割後仍殘留在農產品上，再被人類與動物食用。有些化學藥品，如滴滴涕 (DDT)，與多種疾病及發展失調有關。添加劑的使用也引起關切。添加物是加在食物中用以保持其新鮮度或改變色澤的化學物質。雖然添加物不會造成立即的食物中毒，但為人詬病的是易造成過敏、荷爾蒙失調、消化系統問題及癌症。

　　為了吃更安全的食物，許多人開始吃不含化學物質且環保的有機農產品。而且，像美國食品藥物管理局與英國食品標準局等組織也開始改善食品標籤，確保消費者對於自己吃的食品獲得足夠的資訊。在他們的努力下，人們可以更聰明地購買商品。希望有一天我們可以免於食物恐懼。

解析

1. 本篇文章主旨在於講述因為基因改造技術與化學物質的應用，使得 **(B)** 人們對於自己食用的食物充滿不安全感。
2. 根據第二段第四句、第三段第二句與第六句的敘述可得知 (A)、(B)、(C) 三者都有在文章中被提及，故本題答案為 **(D)**。
3. 由第二段倒數第一句與第二句作者接連提出基改食物是否會造成對人體健康的傷害來看，作者對於基改食物抱持著 **(A)** 懷疑的態度。
4. 第三段 **❻** 提到食品添加劑雖未造成立即性的食物中毒，但卻會引起過敏、荷爾蒙失調、消化系統問題與癌症。
5. 第四段第二句提到美國食品藥物管理局致力於改善食品標籤以確保消費者對於自己購買的食品獲得足夠的資訊來判斷其安全性，故本題 **(D)** 的敘述有誤。

controversy　n.　爭議	potentially　adv.　可能地	selective　adj.　選擇性的
transfer　v.　轉移	for instance　例如	freeze　v.　結冰
allergy　n.　過敏反應	severe　adj.　十分嚴重的	pesticide　n.　殺蟲劑
various　adj.　各式各樣的	developmental　adj.　發展的	digestive　adj.　消化的
organic　adj.　有機的	label　v.　貼標籤	effort　n.　努力

忙得沒時間打理健康

　　大部分的人都知道自己沒有做足夠的運動,但是他們會一直告訴自己:「下星期我會開始運動健身。」可想而知,他們下禮拜還是會很忙碌,於是就延到下下星期,然後是下下下星期。事實上,現代人的生活非常忙碌,我們很難找出時間來保持健康。

　　相較之下,這是現代社會才有的問題,因為在好幾年前,身體健康是生活的一部分。人們走路去上學、工作,或是騎腳踏車去,而且距離通常很長。此外,很多人從事種田,在陽光下及新鮮的空氣中鍛鍊他們的肌肉。這些耗時的日常瑣事是生活的一部分。這些健壯勞動者的後代,可能是在辦公室裡工作,在桌子前坐上一整天。午餐時,他們忙得沒有時間吃健康的餐點。接著下班之後,他們走到停車的地方開車回家,然後就一直坐在電視機前,直到他們上床睡覺。這樣不活躍且飲食高熱量的生活方式,導致人們肥胖、心臟病,或是早死的例子增加。

　　那麼針對這個健康危機,我們能做些什麼呢?首先,若路程不長,人們可以開始以騎腳踏車或走路來代替開車。另外,人們可以習慣性地從辦公桌前站起來伸展。根據調查顯示,每天只要 30 分鐘的激烈運動就能保持健康。「每次都爬樓梯,永遠不要搭電梯。」一位訓練奧運國手的日本教練,被問到要如何保持身材時這麼說。你也可以在下班以後,花短短的時間在家附近散散步,並鼓勵孩子從事真正的運動,而不要總是玩遊戲機。每個小小改變,將會讓你獲得一個更健康的身體,或許還能讓你更加長壽。

解析

1. 本篇文章的關鍵字為運動,主旨在於 **(C)** 闡述運動的重要性並且提供一些運動的建議。
2. 第二段最後一句提到不活躍且飲食高熱量的生活方式可能會提高肥胖、心臟病與早死的可能性,故本題只有 **(D)** 飢餓未被提及。
3. 根據第二段第七句的敘述,**(C)** 人們下班後就開車回家是一種不活躍的生活模式,因此無助於保持體態。
4. 第三段 ❹ 提到要保持好身材的祕訣就是每天進行 30 分鐘的激烈運動。
5. 根據第三段第五句的敘述,這位日本奧運國手的教練是以爬樓梯取代搭乘電梯的方式來保持體態,故本題 **(B)** 的敘述有誤。

postpone v. 延後	modern adj. 現代的	relatively adv. 相對地
fitness n. 健康	chore n. 日常瑣事	descendant n. 後代
occasionally adv. 有時	crisis n. 危機	for one thing (原因) 其一
stretch v. 伸展	vigorous adj. 劇烈的	elevator n. 電梯
neighborhood n. 街區	engage in 參與	pay off 取得好結果

跨閱英文

王信雲 編著　　車昀庭 審定

學習不限於書本上的知識，而是「**跨**」出去，學習帶得走的能力！

跨文化
呈現不同的國家或文化，進而了解及尊重多元文化。

跨世代
橫跨時間軸，經歷不同的世代，見證其發展里程碑。

跨領域
整合兩個或兩個以上領域之間的知識，拓展知識領域。

1. 以新課綱的核心素養為主軸
網羅 3 大面向──「跨文化」、「跨世代」、「跨領域」，共 24 篇文章，引發你對各項議題的好奇。包含多元文化、家庭、生涯規劃、科技、資訊、性別平等、生命、閱讀素養、戶外、環境、海洋、防災等之多項重要議題，開拓多元領域的視野！

2. 跨出一板一眼的作答舒適圈
以循序漸進的實戰演練，搭配全彩的圖像設計，引導學生跳脫形式學習，練出「混合題型」新手感，並更進一步利用「進階練習」的訓練，達到整合知識和活用英文的能力。最後搭配「延伸活動」，讓你在各式各樣的活動中 *FUN* 學英文！

3. 隨書附贈活動式設計解析本
自學教學兩相宜，方便你完整對照中譯，有效理解文章，並有詳細的試題解析，讓你擊破各個答題關卡，從容應試每一關！

英閱百匯

車昀庭　審閱
蘇文賢　審訂
三民英語編輯小組　彙編

本書依據教育部提出之性別平等、人權、環境、海洋教育等多項議題撰寫 36 回仿大考、英檢及多益閱讀測驗文章。文章揉合各式各樣閱讀媒材、模式，讓你在攻克英文閱讀測驗同時也能閱讀生活中的英文。

掌握108課綱大考趨勢
充分練習混合題

5 大主題 ┃ 50 篇文章

生態
物種

人文
歷史

醫學
保健

素養
＋
議題

環境
保育

科學
科技

- 題目參照大考中心命題方向設計，充分練習混合題。
- 隨書附贈翻譯與解析夾冊，方便練習後閱讀文章中譯
  及試題解析，並補充每回文章精選的 15 個字彙。

「英文閱讀High Five」
與「翻譯與解析」不分售
19-80647G